"I'm sorry. Didn't mean to startle you. The Jingle Bell Bomber made it quite clear I couldn't contact you or anyone before I came." Zac set his bomb kit bag down.

"JB sent you and Ziva to help me find this bomb?"

"He said that I couldn't tell anyone or evacuate the building or he'd blow it and more people would die." He paused. Should he tell her the rest? "He also told me you and your parents would die if I didn't obey."

Her hand flew to her mouth. Her eyes glistened. "It's like he knows us...somehow. He called me Olly."

Zac's breath hitched. When Zac and Olly had been together, only her family and close friends—along with him—used her nickname. "Could be a coincidence." He didn't believe in those. The Jingle Bell Bomber had targeted them both for a reason. Why?

"But why you and not the Ottawa police?"

A question Zac had asked. "He said, 'My reasons are my own. Just follow the rules or more people will die.'"

Darlene L. Turner is an award-winning author who lives with her husband, Jeff, in Ontario, Canada. Her love of suspense began when she read her first Nancy Drew book. She's turned that passion into her writing and believes readers will be captured by her plots, inspired by her strong characters and moved by her inspirational message. Visit Darlene at www.darlenelturner.com, where there's suspense beyond borders.

Books by Darlene L. Turner

Love Inspired Suspense

Border Breach
Abducted in Alaska
Lethal Cover-Up
Safe House Exposed
Fatal Forensic Investigation
Explosive Christmas Showdown

Visit the Author Profile page at LoveInspired.com.

EXPLOSIVE CHRISTMAS SHOWDOWN

DARLENE L. TURNER

LOVE INSPIRED SUSPENSE

INSPIRATIONAL ROMANCE

Love Inspired® SUSPENSE

INSPIRATIONAL ROMANCE

ISBN-13: 978-1-335-58807-4

Recycling programs
for this product may
not exist in your area.

Explosive Christmas Showdown

Copyright © 2022 by Darlene L. Turner

For questions and comments about the quality of this book, please contact us
at CustomerService@Harlequin.com.

Love Inspired
22 Adelaide St. West, 41st Floor
Toronto, Ontario M5H 4E3, Canada
www.LoveInspired.com

Printed in U.S.A.

And we know that all things work together for good to them that love God, to them who are the called according to his purpose.
—*Romans* 8:28

For my nieces and nephews.
You bless my life.

ONE

"Someone will die in your office today."

CI analyst Olive Wells gripped her cell phone tighter and halted at the entrance of the federal police headquarters in Ottawa, Ontario. "Who's this?" An icy wind swirled around her neck and she tugged her plaid scarf closer to block out both the snowy day and her jackhammering heartbeat thundering through her head.

"Who do you think? Just call me JB for short." The caller's distorted voice indicated he'd used a changer app to disguise his identity. A throaty, evil laugh rumbled over top of "Jingle Bells" booming through the cell phone. "Let's play a game, shall we?" The music on her phone stopped.

Olive gulped. The Jingle Bell Bomber had somehow gotten access to her unlisted cell phone number. Thoughts of the serial bomber threatening her region circled in her mind. Earlier, her leader had announced at a unit meeting that Olive would lead the Criminal Investigative Analysis team in providing the profile to catch the Jingle Bell Bomber. *No pressure.* She pushed through the door and scrambled to the security desk, waving her hand to get the officer's attention. She muted her cell phone. "Trace this call," she whispered. "Serial bomber on the line." Normally she'd get a warrant, but the exigent circumstance justified her request.

"On it." Constable Bracken bolted upright and clicked his radio, asking for a trace on Olive's cell phone.

She unmuted her phone.

"Are you still there, Olly?"

Olive shuddered. His use of her nickname implied JB knew her personally. Or was it just an educated guess?

Something she refused to do. Guesses in her line of work could mean life or death.

"Santa Baby" played over her building's speaker system, interrupting her thoughts. The Christmas tree lights in the foyer's corner flickered in syncopation as if mocking her fear. "I'm here. What do you want from me?"

"I like Mariah's version of that song better." A pause followed by a menacing snicker sailed through the phone. "Get to your cubicle or I will detonate the bomb right now."

She bypassed the elevator and hustled to the

stairs. She didn't want to risk getting cut off. "Why me? Do I know you?" She had to keep him talking. Find out more to include in her profile and give her colleagues time to trace the call. She hurried up the steps.

"Trying to psychoanalyze me? Trace this call? It won't work. You have exactly thirty minutes to find my Christmas present."

"I'm not qualified. I need to call in the bomb unit."

"Don't even think about it. You do that and I will set it off. Only you and a special someone I sent your way can play my Jingle Bell game."

What? Who was he referring to? She reached her floor, opened the door and stopped to catch her breath. A thought entered her mind. She must get someone else's attention. Her boss. She turned left toward his office.

"Olly, you're going the wrong way. Your cubicle is in the other direction."

She sucked in a breath.

"That's right. I can see you."

She pivoted and spots danced in her vision as the room swayed. *Breathe. You can do this.* She braced herself against a wall and looked at the hall camera, scowling.

"Tsk-tsk. Turn your frown upside down." He laughed. "By the way, you look pretty in green."

She grimaced and resisted the urge to catch

an officer's attention. "How did you get access to our video cameras? This is a secure building." Olive walked toward her work area, bent on obeying JB's rules. Her desire to protect innocent lives trumped her fears. The bomber had already killed two people, one of them a police officer in her hometown of Stittsrock Falls—twenty minutes from Canada's capital—and where she still lived today. She couldn't bring herself to live in a large city. Stittsrock Falls' population of twenty thousand suited her fine. Thankfully her boss had approved her working from home full-time with occasional in-person meetings in Ottawa. Like today. JB's case had warranted extra in-person team collaboration.

"Let's just say I spend much of my time alone," JB said.

Loner. Probably lives by himself or with his mother. Male, mid-thirties. Polite. Olive silently ticked the boxes to include on her profile. She'd been reading up on famous serial bombers in the past forty-eight hours. What was JB's motive? Revenge? Political?

"Morning, Olive," Lauren Trotter said. "See the boss put you in charge on this one, huh?" Her fellow CI analyst's lips flattened.

Lauren had had it in for Olive ever since Olive's profiling had helped her sister Scarlet catch the Coastline Strangler. Her boss had praised Olive's work in front of everyone, promoted her, given her the largest cubicle, and approved her working from Stittsrock Falls.

However, she had seniority over the rookie analyst. Something Lauren tried hard to ignore.

"Step away from the pretty blonde," JB said. "Time to start our game. Go to your desk."

"Morning, Lauren." Olive raised her cell phone. "I gotta take this important call. Chat later."

"Good girl." JB's sarcastic tone sounded through the phone.

Olive struggled to curb her heightened heartbeat as she stepped into her spacious corner cube by the window. She tossed her purse on her desk and wiggled out of her coat. "Listen here, don't you dare put all these people at risk. Why target us? What did we do to you?"

"Temper, temper. It's simple, your department is getting in my way. I can't have that."

"Why are you killing people?" Olive jiggled her mouse to bring her computer to life. She wanted to take notes to help get the profile right.

"That's not on today's agenda. Okay, here's how the game will work. You have thirty minutes to find the Christmas present. You can't tell anyone what you're doing or tip off any other officers to the danger. Only the man on his way to see you can play. If you engage anyone else, I will find out and you will pay."

Olive's laptop dinged. A message from Constable Bracken. "The call is pinging off multiple cell towers. Keep him talking."

The team required more time.

"What man?" she asked.

"You'll find out soon enough."

She wanted more information. "You killed a postal worker and a police officer. What's the connection between the two?"

"Maybe there's one and maybe there isn't. You didn't think I'd make the game easy, did you?"

A question entered her mind. "Do you hate Christmas? Is that why you started bombing now?"

A dog barked close by.

Her pulse elevated. Ever since a dog attacked her at age twelve and left a scar on the bridge of her nose, she was terrified of them.

"Aw…your help has arrived. Let the game begin. Remember the rules," JB warned as "Jingle Bells" played briefly before the call clicked off.

A knock sounded on her cubicle's metal wall.

She rose to her feet and came face-to-face with the man who'd broken her heart.

Constable Zac Turner, her ex-fiancé, and his K-9 partner Ziva stood outside her work area.

Olive's phone slipped from her fingers. Ignoring the sudden rush of emotions, she inhaled sharply and squared her shoulders. For the sake of everyone inside the building, she had to work with the last person she wanted to see right now.

You can do this.

Stittsrock Falls' Constable Zac Turner's jaw dropped at Olly's reaction to their presence. The Jingle Bell Bomber had called him and ordered him to get to her office to play his game. No other players allowed. He'd advised his leader that a confidential informant in Ottawa had requested a meet. Zac hated secrets, but he had to follow the rules—or else. He wouldn't put her life or her coworkers' lives at risk. However, JB had said nothing about leaving Ziva behind. Zac's trusty chocolate Lab would help to locate the bomb quickly. She'd been trained in explosives detection, while stationary and moving, plus search and rescue. The dual-purpose K-9 had already gained a positive reputation for herself.

But Olly's ashen face told him she was not pleased to see them.

"Ziva, sit," Zac commanded.

She obeyed.

He addressed Olly. "I'm sorry. Didn't mean to startle you. The Jingle Bell Bomber made it quite clear I couldn't contact you or anyone before I came." Zac set his bomb kit bag down.

Olly scooped her phone off the floor. "JB sent you and Ziva to help me find this bomb?"

"Well, technically, he said nothing about Ziva. Only that I couldn't tell anyone or evacuate the building, or he'd blow it and more people would die. No winning solution here." He paused. Should he tell her the rest? He raked his fingers through his short hair. "He also told me you and your parents would die if I didn't obey."

Her hand flew to her mouth, but not in time to squelch her cry. Her eyes glistened. "I don't understand, Zac. It's like he knows us…somehow. He called me Olly."

Zac's breath hitched at the bomber's use of her nickname. When Zac and Olly were together, only her family and close friends—along with him—used it. "Could be a coincidence." He didn't believe in those. The Jingle Bell Bomber had targeted them both for a reason. Why?

"But why you and not the Ottawa police?"

A question Zac had asked. "He said, 'My reasons are my own. Just follow the rules or more people will die.'" The last words JB had spoken before hanging up.

Olly peered at her watch. "We have twenty-five minutes. Impossible to get through the building so quick."

"Some game, huh? He probably doesn't expect us to win, but what he didn't count on was Ziva here."

Ziva's ears raised at the mention of her name.

"How will we get her to search without arousing suspicion? JB is watching somehow through our cameras. Plus, everyone will want to know what a dog is doing in the building."

Zac tapped his chin. "We need a cover story. Quick."

She chewed on a strand of her brown hair. "We'll pretend I'm showing you around the building. That you're currently training her."

"Yes, let's go." Zac picked up his duffel bag and turned to his Lab. "Ziva, come."

Ziva got up and waited. The dog knew from Zac's tone it was time to get to work.

Zac walked around her work area and stopped.

Olly lagged and approached cautiously. Was she still scared of dogs?

He ignored his silent question and focused on his K-9. "Ziva, seek." He unhooked her leash.

Ziva trotted down the hall, moving back and forth while pausing to sniff.

A pretty blonde stood from her desk. "Olive, what's going on?"

Olly inched closer to Zac. "Nothing much. Just helping Zac train Ziva in an office setting with staff around. Nothing to be concerned about. Did you get the bomb crime scene pictures?"

"Good answer," Zac mumbled. She was good at thinking on her feet.

"Yes, boss." The woman laced the word *boss* with sarcasm. "Sending them to you now."

Ziva wandered farther down the hall. "Time to follow her," Zac said.

Olly nodded and walked in step with Zac.

He gestured toward the coworker. "Wow, she doesn't seem to like you, does she?"

"That's an understatement. Ever since I got promoted, Lauren has had it in for me."

"She's just jealous."

Ziva walked into an office, bringing Zac's attention back to the game. "I think she's found something."

"What's going on here?" a voice boomed from the room Ziva entered.

"Great, that's my boss's office," Olly said. "This should be interesting."

The pair jogged into the room.

Ziva crisscrossed through the large office and back out into the hall before returning to the room and circling the small Christmas tree. She sniffed the gifts and finally sat next to the large one at the back.

Her alert cue.

Zac turned to Olly. "She's found something."

"Sergeant, sorry for the intrusion," Olly said. "Can you leave your office, please?"

The balding man stood and fisted his hands on his hips. "Not until you tell me what's going on. Why is there a dog sniffing around? And why is your ex-fiancé here?"

"Sergeant Alexander, I will explain everything later. Please leave the room."

His eyes narrowed. "Fine, but there better be a good explanation." He stomped out.

"You too, Olive." Zac retrieved Ziva's ball from his pocket and rewarded her behavior. "Ziva, good girl. Stay."

She caught her toy, wagging her tail and rested in the entrance.

Olly widened her stance. "I'm not going anywhere. We have to get rid of the bomb before it goes off. Can you do that? I know you've worked in your bomb unit."

The expression on her pretty face revealed she was not budging. If he remembered anything from their time together, when she made up her mind, there was no stopping her. "Stand in the corner."

Zac put on his gloves before inching over to the gift. A note attached to a bow read "Open me." Zac took a mirror tool from his bag that would help him see under the box's lid. He moved it around, checking for any booby-trap wires.

"Okay, nothing. Opening it now." He gulped and gently lifted the lid.

A metal pipe and a piece of paper with the word *Boom* lay inside, along with a canister. Using the mirror, Zac peeked inside the canister. After close inspection, he let out the breath he'd been holding and sat back on his heels, hauling out the clear container. "It's a fake."

Olly walked to his side. "Are you sure?"

He held up the canister. "Yes, this is smokeless powder we use in training detector dogs. This is what Ziva smelled." He lifted out the pipe. A jingle bell ornament lay under it along with an envelope, "Olly" typed on it. He gritted his teeth; JB had targeted her. He removed an evidence bag and dropped the note into it before placing it in his duffel bag. "It's addressed to you, but we need to dust for fingerprints first."

Both their phones chimed as "Jingle Bells" blared through the building's speakers.

Ziva discarded her toy and jumped up.

He peered at the text message on his phone.

You cheated and now someone will die.

Zac's heart rate kicked into overdrive as he shouldered his bag. There were more bombs.

"Ziva, seek!"

The dog dashed from the room.

Seconds later, an explosion rocked the floor, followed by the sound of shattering glass.

They were under attack from the Jingle Bell Bomber's deadly game.

The gift had been a decoy, and Zac had to secure the building before more bombs were unleashed.

TWO

Olive's breath labored in the smoke-filled corridor. She resisted the urge to wipe her eyes. It would only irritate them further. The bomb had damaged the other side of her floor. Her boots crunched on fallen glass as she and Zac combed the area looking for any hurt coworkers and Ziva. The K-9 had taken off in the bomb's direction moments before the explosion, and the pinched expression on Zac's face told her he worried about his dog.

She grazed his arm. "She's okay. We'll find her. God's got this." She believed that with all her heart, though lately she'd been questioning whether God heard her prayers. The man beside her was one of those pleas.

Six months after he had proposed, he'd broken off their engagement, stating their relationship wouldn't work out. That, combined with the fact she never wanted to birth a child of her own, had propelled her into a vow of remaining single—forever.

Before totally committing her life to Christ, she had become pregnant in college, but miscarried on Christmas Day and had almost died. That had sent her into a blur of disbelief, sparking her fear of getting pregnant. She still longed for motherhood, and God had recently answered her prayer about fostering a child. Grace Patterson arrived three months ago and Olive had already fallen in love with the six-year-old.

Zac nodded. "Ziva! Where are you? Come on, girl, talk to me."

A distant bark resonated on the floor.

"Someone help!" a muffled female voice yelled from down the hall in the same direction.

"That's Lauren. This way." Olive dodged debris and walked through the hole in an office wall to get to Lauren's distressed callout position.

Ziva's barking increased in volume and Olive stopped in her tracks, her chest tightening. Would the dog hurt her?

"What is it, Olive?" Zac asked.

Should she remind him of her fear of dogs? Not that she didn't like them; she was just terrified ever since her attack. Many of her schoolmates had laughed at her fear. Even counseling sessions hadn't helped ease her anxiety.

Lauren's cry brought her out of her state.

"I'm good." She mustered courage and pressed forward toward Ziva and the woman.

Moments later, they reached Lauren and the object of her distress. Rick, a fellow employee, lay motionless under fallen debris. Lauren stood off to his side in some sort of shocked stupor. Ziva sat beside the woman and nudged her hand.

Was the dog trying to comfort Lauren?

Olive scurried to her coworker's side. "Rick, can you hear me?"

Silence.

Zac dropped his bag and hauled the chunk of drywall off Rick.

Olive knelt and placed her fingers on his neck, hoping to find a pulse. "He's gone."

"No!" Lauren squatted beside Olive.

Zac walked to Ziva and stroked the chocolate Lab's head. "Good girl. So glad you're safe."

"Sh-she…saved. My. Life," Lauren stammered. "If it wasn't for her, I would be under all that debris."

"What happened?" Zac asked.

"I was about to go into Rick's office when your dog tugged me backward. Seconds later, the explosion took out the entranceway." Lauren bit her lip as tears fell, creating a trail through her soot-smudged cheeks.

Zac pointed to Rick's office. "What was his role here?"

"Head of Forensics." Olive tilted her head. "Why his office? You think JB targeted him specifically? But why—"

Zac placed his index finger on his lips, suggesting she stop talking.

Right. The game.

Smoke swirled into the corridor. The explosion had also started a fire, but so far, it was contained to the office. "Zac, can you get the extinguisher on the wall? We have to put out the flames before they spread."

Zac quickly sprayed the area, leaving smoke burning her nose and eyes.

Pounding footsteps caught her attention and she turned in their direction. Her leader. What had taken him so long to get to them?

Sergeant Alexander approached. "What happened? Is everyone okay?"

More employees congregated in the hall, curiosity bringing them to their floor's corner.

"Explosion in Rick's office." Olive motioned her boss away from Lauren. She didn't need the woman going into hysterics with what Olive was about to say. "We need to evacuate the building, sir. This bomb was isolated, but there could be more."

Zac stepped next to her. "She's right. We don't know what we're dealing with."

"I called for emergency services. They're on

their way." Sergeant Alexander pointed to the mess. "How do you know all this?"

Olive averted her gaze to Zac. It would be hard to keep this game from her sergeant and she was at a loss as to what to do. Tell him and risk more bombs going off? Or somehow bring him into the loop?

Zac gave his head a slight nod.

Olive turned back to her boss. "Sir, do you trust me?"

"Of course."

She moved closer. "Can't talk here." She gestured toward the camera.

Sergeant Ike Alexander's eyes followed her gaze. "Understood. Later." He clapped. "Everyone, time to evacuate our floor. Standard procedure. Firefighters and paramedics are en route. Leave through the east stairwell."

"I. Can't. Leave. Him." Lauren's words came between sobs.

Olive gathered Lauren into her arms. "He's gone. I'm so sorry, but we have to leave. It's not safe here."

A light fixture clattered to the floor, confirming her words.

"Don't worry. Others will be here shortly to take him away."

Olive's cell phone chimed. She ignored it and

helped Lauren to her feet. "Go with the sergeant, okay?"

Sergeant Alexander wrapped his arm around Lauren and guided her to the exit.

Others ran by them, following the group headed to safety.

"We need to search the rest of the floor, just in case—" Their chiming cell phones interrupted Zac's words.

Olive's senses heightened at what she guessed was about to happen. She read the text.

The game isn't over.

She glanced at Zac.

His eyes widened as he checked the joint text.

There were more bombs in the building, and it was up to them to find them.

"Ziva, seek!" Zac wrapped his bag's strap across his body and opened the door leading to the other floors.

The K-9 darted down the stairs. Had she picked up a scent on a lower level?

Zac turned to Olly. "Stay close behind me. Ziva would have found other bombs in this area, if there were any. Time to search the rest of the floors. I don't want you out of my sight."

Her lips flattened. "I can take care of myself. I took extra defensive training."

Zac didn't have time to argue. Her stubborn streak had always frustrated him, but her strong will and brave attitude impressed him at the same time. "I know you can. Come on, let's follow Ziva." He squared his shoulders, determination setting in. Not only would he protect Olive Wells, but everyone in this building. Even if it cost him his life.

They burst through the first-floor doors, letting Ziva lead them office to office. So far, she hadn't alerted to any scents.

Zac's radio crackled and his boss's voice boomed through the speaker. "Turner, an Ottawa police officer is requesting to speak with you. He saw our K-9 vehicle in the parking lot and called me. When you get back into town, we have to talk. Switch to Channel 5."

Zac winced. He was in trouble, but it couldn't be helped. He changed the channel and pressed the button. "Constable Turner. Who's this?"

"Ottawa police. Constable Spearing here. I've been told you're clearing the floors with your K-9. Our bomb unit is here to assist."

Olly yanked on his arm. "We can't bring them in," she whispered.

"JB would realize by now someone notified the Ottawa police, and we'd evacuate," Zac said to Olly. "We have to take the risk. We need their help."

"I don't like it. He could set off another bomb."

"I have a funny feeling that's been his intent all along." He pressed his radio button. "We're on the first level and already checked the second. Have your team conduct a thorough search on the remaining floors."

"Copy that."

Thirty minutes after his K-9 cleared the first floor, Olly, Zac and Ziva walked out into the snowy day and joined the rest of her colleagues huddled by a tree in the front of the building.

Olly rubbed her arms. "It's freezing out here. We have to get everyone back inside."

"Not until the bomb unit clears the rest of the floors." Zac shrugged out of his coat. "Here, this will help." He wrapped his police-issued jacket around her shoulders and didn't miss her cinnamon-scented perfume. He hesitated to breathe in the familiar aroma. It brought too much pain. He'd had no choice but to break up with her after he'd discovered his real identity. His mob boss father had ruined any shot of him ever having a relationship. Zac wouldn't put Olly or any other woman in danger from the ruthless mobster bent on destroying anyone in Zac's life.

He shuffled out of her personal space, distancing himself from further hurt.

Ziva barked, bringing him from his self-pitying fog.

Zac followed the dog's gaze. Another K-9 trotted out of the building along with his handler. The officer carried a Christmas present. The German shepherd had obviously found a gift from JB on another floor.

Zac stiffened. A decoy? Was another bomb about to explode?

He and Olly jogged toward the officer.

"What did you find?" Zac asked.

The younger man held up the box. "Fake bomb. Note is addressed to Constable Zac Turner from the Stittsrock Falls Police Department."

"That's me." Zac exhaled. Maybe JB had only been teasing that the game wasn't over. Although his gut told him otherwise. No time to let his guard down.

"However, I can't give this to you. Forensics will dust for prints."

"Understood. I will need it after, though, for an ongoing investigation." Zac handed him his business card. "Please have someone call me when you've finished with the present. Can I take a picture of the note since it's addressed to me?"

"I guess." The officer opened the box.

Zac quickly took a picture. He would compare it to the one addressed to Olly, which was still safely stowed in his bag.

Other officers and K-9s left the building.

"Are we good to reenter?" Olly asked.

"Our unit has cleared the rest of the floors and the firefighters have put out any remaining embers," the constable said. "However, I would wait until your employers have given the all-clear as per your building's evacuation procedures."

"Thank you, Officer." Zac guided Olly and Ziva away from the man. "I think we should retrieve any of your documentation and get your team to a secure location."

Olly's eyes widened. "What? You don't think we'll be safe at headquarters?"

"Do you, after today? The building has eyes, so to speak. Plus, it's clear to me JB has targeted you and your team. You're not safe in there."

"Good point. Let me talk to Sergeant Alexander."

"I'll also reach out to my leader. He's probably guessed I misinformed him about why I was in Ottawa."

Three hours later, Zac, Olly and her Criminal Investigative Analysis team members Lauren Trotter and Fraser Graham sat around a table in a safe house located in the woods on the outskirts of the city. Her sergeant had stayed behind to check on the status of their headquarters, but would join them later.

The team had picked up pizza on the way after

gathering their laptops and belongings from the cleared floor. Zac had retrieved the fake bomb they'd discovered before the explosion. Only Olly's team and her leader knew their location. They planned to keep it that way until they could regroup after today's Jingle Bell game.

Ziva chewed contentedly on a bone in the corner.

Olly changed rooms to make a personal phone call. She was secretive about it, but when she emerged, a radiant smile illuminated her face.

Had she called a boyfriend? Jealousy punched him in the gut. *Stop, Turner. She's no longer yours and won't be. Let. Her. Go.*

Zac finished his slice of pepperoni pizza and inspected the metal pipe JB had planted in the Christmas box. Another jingle bell ornament lay underneath. Obviously, part of the bomber's signature. Zac retrieved his magnifying glass and slowly examined the metal. He stopped when he came upon a strange etching. "Olive, come and look at this."

She peered over his shoulder. "What is it?"

He pointed. "Check out the crude drawing."

Olly leaned closer and inhaled sharply. "It's a jingle bell with JB carved beside it. His signature."

Lauren popped out of her chair. "Let me see."

She nudged Olly out of the way and moved closer to Zac.

Too close for his liking.

Olly's scowl told him she agreed.

Fraser had settled in a rocking chair, scouring police documents. Olly's boss had hand-picked the two analysts to work with her in developing the Jingle Bell Bomber's profile. They'd realized they must work in seclusion, as somehow the bomber had tapped into their office's surveillance equipment. Sergeant Alexander had also reported they had discovered a virus in their computer system. It was the only answer as to how JB had accessed their feeds.

A knock banged, startling him.

Zac's hand flew to his sidearm and he positioned himself to the door's right.

"It's Ike," Olly's boss called from behind the door. "I have the rest of the evidence."

The group expelled a simultaneous breath.

Zac opened the door and the man stepped inside, stomping his boots. "It's coming down hard now."

Olly held out her hand. "Did you get the letter?"

He nodded and passed it to her. "They dusted for prints. Forensics will let me know what they find. Also, Constable Bracken said they failed to get JB's location from pinging his cell phone."

Zac flipped to the picture he'd taken of the note addressed to him. "Let's compare the two notes. What does yours say?"

Olly opened the folded note. "It's typed. Looks like from an old typewriter. Odd. Says—" She gasped.

"What is it, Olly?"

Her gaze snapped to his at the use of her nickname.

He cringed. *Oops.*

Olly cleared her throat. "'Make sure you follow the rules or Grace will pay the price.'" She bit her lip. "How does he know my personal information?"

Good question and who's Grace?

Zac peered at the picture of the note addressed to him. With everything that had happened, he hadn't read it yet.

I will get to them all and you can't stop me. The next game play will be close to your home, Zac. Plus, you and Olly will pay for your sins, so beware and watch your backs. You're also on my naughty list.

Signed, The JB Bomber

Sins? What sins? Zac's anxiety levels increased, locking his muscles. How were Olly and

Zac connected to the Jingle Bell Bomber? Zac eyed Olly and read the trepidation on her contorted, pretty face. He vowed to himself to stay close to her. For some odd reason, JB had targeted them all and her life was in danger.

Right now, Zac had to get back to Stittsrock Falls before more bombs exploded and killed residents of his beloved hometown.

THREE

"Chief Bennett, is that wise? We're not sure what JB is capable of, so should we move the team to our station house? We'll put everyone at risk." Zac had called his leader after receiving the threatening note from JB. It was clear the next part of the bomber's plan was in Stittsrock Falls and required Zac to bring the chief up to speed. He couldn't keep it a secret any longer—it hit too close to home.

His and Olly's.

Zac prayed JB wouldn't penalize him for breaking the rules. Prayed? When was the last time he'd reached out to God? He and Olly had gone to church together when they were dating, but lately he'd only been a holiday-church-going type of Christian. His mother hadn't raised him that way, so when had it changed?

You know when.

The day he'd discovered his real name—real identity.

His mother had taken sick and he'd been searching through her drawers for her medication, but what he'd found had rocked his world. His birth certificate.

Devin Burns—son of the infamous British Columbia mob boss, Harry Burns.

Zac had stumbled back to the living room where his mother rested and demanded the truth. She'd confessed to naïvely falling in love with the man, getting married and pregnant—all before realizing her husband's true identity. He was the ruthless mobster wanted across Canada. When she had confronted Harry, he had beaten her and threatened that if she left, he'd find her and kill them both. Plus, anyone else close to them. She'd realized then that she had to leave. It was a risk worth taking to get away from the man's clutches, so she'd fled in the middle of the night, driving across Canada to find a secluded town. His mother had finally settled on Stittsrock Falls and legally changed their identities. She'd told no one the truth.

It was when he'd learned about his father's identity that Zac had lost his faith in Christ. He'd questioned how goodness could coexist with evil and if God really worked out everything for good in their lives. After studying his father's arrest record and the multiple times he had threatened his family throughout the years, he'd known then he would have to break up with Olly. He wasn't willing to put her or her family in mortal danger.

Nobody knew Zac's real identity. He hated secrets, but he had no choice. He had to stay hidden from his father and protect everyone around him.

"Turner, you there?" The chief's angry voice jolted Zac back to the present.

He massaged his tense shoulder muscle. "Sorry, Chief."

"We're police. We put our lives on the line every day. This bomber has targeted you both for a reason. It sounds like JB probably lives in our area. Is there anyone you know who might be the bomber?"

Zac racked his brain, thinking of those in the community. "No one I can imagine doing anything remotely like this. I'll talk to Olive. Something might trigger once we get her team's official profile on the Jingle Bell Bomber."

"Sounds good. I'll tell our team and prepare for your arrival."

"Chief, I think we should put the team up in a secluded place not associated with our station and not a hotel."

Fingers drumming on a desk roared through the phone. Something Zac came to recognize as Chief Bennett's way of thinking. "Okay. I'll find a place big enough for all of you. Safety in numbers."

Zac flinched. Would Olly agree? He doubted she'd want to be around him 24/7. "Can you have patrol cars monitor our families as well?"

"On it. See you soon. Drive safe. It's nasty out there." Chief Bennett clicked off the call.

Zac walked from the room where he'd phoned his chief in private and stepped into the kitchen. The group had papers spread out over the table, studying them closely.

"Olive and Sergeant Alexander, can I speak to you both?" He gestured them to follow him into the living room.

Ziva lay curled next to the fireplace, sleeping. She stirred at Zac's presence and raised her ears.

He stroked the Lab's head. "You're a good girl."

Olly positioned herself at the opposite side of the room and leaned against the wall. "What is it, Zac?"

Wow. You really do like to distance yourself from me. Not that he blamed her reserved attitude after how he'd broken it off. He'd probably do the same. He still hated himself for having to end things so mysteriously. Would she ever forgive him? Would he forgive himself?

Her boss entered. "Zac, call me Ike. What's going on?"

"I just got off the phone with my chief. Since your floor is in rough shape and it appears JB is moving his game to Stittsrock Falls, Chief Bennett suggests your team come to our station to set up shop and give us your profile. Plus, we have an exceptional bomb unit led by Constable Pike. He can be prickly, but he's efficient in defusing bombs." He left out the part where they'd all be staying in one place for safety reasons. Best to leave that for later. Ease her into it.

Olly shot away from the wall, straightening her posture. "Is that really necessary? We have other areas in the building we could set up, plus lots of protection."

Sergeant Alexander raised his hand. "Just wait, Olive. I spoke to my superiors earlier, and they're concerned about how JB got into our system. This is a good idea. I want you, Lauren and Fraser to pack up the evidence you've gathered and head to Stittsrock Falls. Since you already work from your hometown, the rest of the team can mobilize easily."

Olly once again chewed on a strand of hair, then dropped it as if it scorched her fingers. "But—"

He raised his hand again. "No arguments. Olive, you're good at what you do and I want you to lead this team. Provide a solid profile. We must catch this guy before he kills again."

"Yes, sir. I'm on it." She eyed Ziva.

Something flashed on her pretty face, but Zac

failed to identify the emotion before it disappeared.

"I gotta get back. Stay safe." Sergeant Alexander left.

Zac inched forward. "Listen, Olly—"

"Please don't call me that. It brings too much pain."

He clamped his mouth shut and considered his next words. "I understand, Olive. I didn't mean to hurt you, but I had to protect you—"

He stopped.

You can't tell her or anyone the truth.

She tilted her head, her forehead wrinkling. "Protect me from what?"

"Never mind." Having to keep her safe from JB was enough, but to add the possibility of his identity being leaked would only add fuel to the proverbial fire. "Listen, there's one other thing. The team will stay at an undisclosed, secluded location. We need you all to be safe."

She averted her gaze to the floor. "But it's not just me anymore."

What did that mean?

Olive chewed on her hair. *Ugh!* A habit she'd failed to break even after years of being chastised by her mother. It was what she did when anxiety set in and the thought of having to spend even more time with the man who broke her heart personified her angst, tugging at her heartstrings simultaneously. If that were possible.

Plus, she now had Grace to consider. With a target on Olive's back, how would she keep the six-year-old safe? She had to tell Zac about her foster child.

"I have someone special in my life." She hesitated.

His expression twisted. Was his emotion regret or sadness?

She ignored it and continued. "I now have a foster child living with me."

He let out an audible elongated breath. "Not what I expected you to say. JB referred to a Grace in his note. Is that your foster child?"

The crinkles beside his eyes smiled, catching her attention. She had always loved how his eyes grinned along with his lips. It was her kryptonite when it came to Zac. *Don't do that to me.* Olive dug her nails into her palms to curb any further thoughts of him. "Yes. She's six and came from an abusive situation."

"I remember your soft spot for children. I admire you for giving a child shelter and a home."

"But if I'm sequestered in a safe house, what will happen to her?"

Zac tapped his chin.

The action she remembered as his thinking pose.

"Isn't Constable Skye Lynch a friend of yours?

We can request she be included on the team to protect Grace. The cabin is big enough for everyone. Plus, Ziva would love having a six-year-old around."

"Yes, that could work. Grace loves dogs." If only Olive didn't struggle with being around them because of her attack. *Lord, help my fears to subside.* "Will she be safe at school?"

"I'll check with the chief, but we can have constables patrol her school area."

Olive clenched every muscle in her body.

As if sensing her trepidation, Ziva trotted over to Olive and snuggled next to her, licking her hand.

Olive shuddered, the hairs at the nape of her neck rising.

"She won't bite, you know."

Ziva licked her again.

Olive giggled. "That tickles."

Ziva barked.

Olive started and toppled backward, thudding against the wall. Her heartbeat increased and stole her breath.

Zac grabbed Olive's arm and steadied her. "Ziva, sit." He gestured to the fireplace.

The dog obeyed.

"Are you okay?" he asked.

"She scared me, that's all." Well, more than that. Terrified was a better word, but she wouldn't use it.

"You're still scared of dogs, aren't you?" His lips turned upward.

She nodded and inhaled deeply to slow her heartbeat. "Not just her. All dogs." She folded her arms. "Don't mock me. Aren't you still scared of heights?"

"I am. Sorry, I wasn't mocking, just—"

Lauren bounded into the room. "Guys, you have to see the latest." She pivoted and left as quickly as she came.

Olive brushed by Zac and walked into the kitchen.

Lauren and Fraser huddled in front of Fraser's computer. Lauren beckoned them over. "Look at this."

Zac and Olive stood behind the duo, peering at the screen.

Fraser had paused a news report.

"I follow this station and they posted a video a few minutes ago." Fraser pressed Play.

The white-haired anchorman shuffled papers on his desk. "Breaking news. The Jingle Bell Bomber is claiming responsibility for the bombing at a federal building in Ottawa this morning. A typed message was delivered to us moments ago." He held a piece of paper in the air. "It says, 'The bombing in Ottawa was the next play in my game, but I've only begun. Tomorrow, another person on my list will pay for their actions.' It's signed, JB. Sources tell us one person died in today's bombing, others injured. We'll keep you updated on further developments."

The newscast ended.

Lauren's eyes widened. "What do you think he means by 'another person' on his list?"

"It's our job to find out," Olive said. "My question is what links our victims? That will help identify JB."

Zac crossed his arms. "And why didn't the news station give the police the letter? They've contaminated evidence."

"In their opinion, story obviously trumps protocol." Fraser's laptop dinged, announcing some sort of alert. "Wait, Forensics just sent me an email. Let me check it." He clicked and read. "No prints on either of your notes, so I doubt there would be on the one sent to the news station."

Olive tapped the desk. "Fraser, contact them. I want to see the letter to compare it to ours."

The analyst clicked his cell phone. "On it." He relocated to the living room to make the call.

"What do you want me to do, boss?" Lauren asked.

Olive hated when Lauren called her boss. "We're all heading to Stittsrock Falls to set up at Zac's station and stay in a safe house."

Lauren pursed her lips. "What? I can't leave Ottawa. I have book club tonight."

Zac walked to the window and peered out. "I doubt you do. It's nasty out there. Time to leave now before the weather gets worse. Swing by your homes and pack some belongings. We don't know how long this will take."

"But why Stittsrock Falls?" Lauren stuffed her laptop into her bag.

Olive tugged her coat off the rack. "Because it appears JB has moved his game there."

"And he has targeted your team. It will be safer if we're together." Zac checked his watch. "It's one thirty now. Let's move."

Fraser returned and stopped. "Where are you all going?"

Lauren pointed to Olive. "Her hometown. I'll drive and explain on the way."

"We need to stop at the news station. They agreed to give us the letter." Fraser packed his laptop.

"Be careful and keep your eyes peeled for any suspicious activity." Zac called for Ziva to come. "Let us check the perimeter first and all your cars for bombs. Just in case. I'll text you when it's safe." The duo stepped outside.

A frigid chill snaked into the room and through Olive's body, leaving her with a foreboding question. Was it a sign of things to come?

A few minutes later, her cell phone dinged. Zac gave them the all-clear.

"We're ready. Drive safe." Olive scooped up her laptop bag and left the ranch house.

Zac and Ziva positioned themselves next to Zac's cruiser.

Olive's cell phone rang. She checked the screen. Nigel—a confidential source she'd used in the past. His timing couldn't be worse, but she always trusted his information. She clicked Answer and walked down the veranda steps. "Can't really talk right now, Nigel."

"You're in danger."

She stopped. "What have you heard?"

A distant boom sounded.

Ziva growled then barked before catapulting toward her.

The hair spiked at the back of her neck as visions from her dog attack bull-rushed her. She screamed as Ziva knocked her to the ground and—

A rocket-propelled grenade blasted into her SUV, exploding it to smithereens.

Ziva had saved her life.

Olive's pulse jackknifed into her throat as questions filled her mind.

How had JB discovered their location and how was he staying one step ahead of them at all times?

FOUR

Zac struggled to breathe. The fire from the explosion engulfed Olly's vehicle and sent toxic fumes into the air. He placed his gloved hand over his mouth and stole a breath as best as he could. In. Out. In. Out. Pain stabbed at his knees. The blast had thrown him and knocked him to the icy, snow-covered ground, but right now he only had one concern. Well, two. Where were Olly and Ziva?

He gingerly stood and searched through the smoke. A distant bark reassured him his K-9 was fine. Zac shuffled toward the Lab's cry and that's when he realized what had happened in the split second of the attack.

Olly lay on the ground. Ziva sat beside her, resting her paw on Olly's chest.

Ziva had saved Olly's life.

"Olly!" Zac hurried to her side, forgetting her request not to call her by her nickname. He squatted by her side and caressed her face. *Please, God, help her be okay.*

She wheezed and opened her eyes. She attempted to raise herself up on her elbows, but fell back down.

"Take it easy. Let's get you farther away from the scene." Zac helped Olly to stand and supported her as they moved to the front steps. "Sit here. I'm calling for help. You took the brunt of the blast. Thankfully, your car was parked at the end of the driveway. Ziva must have caught a scent in time and knocked you out of the way."

Hearing her name, Ziva snuggled closer to Olly.

Olly rubbed the dog's head. "Good girl." She leaned against the railing.

The door flung open and Lauren and Fraser appeared at the entrance.

"What happened?" Fraser struggled to get his coat on in the confusion.

"RPG just took out Olive's vehicle." Zac punched 9-1-1 into his phone and requested emergency services, giving them their location.

"But how?" Lauren's eyes widened as she wrapped a scarf around her neck. "Our location was supposed to be a secret."

Good question. Zac wondered the same thing. How had JB found them so quickly? He examined the team's terror-stricken faces. He refused to believe one of them had leaked the information. That left one other possibility.

JB had planted trackers on their vehicles.

Zac raced to his cruiser. He searched the wheel wells, but nothing was lodged under them. He knelt and peered at the undercarriage. A small black box caught his attention. He yanked it out, holding it up.

"This is how he found us. He must have either put it on my cruiser before I left Stittsrock Falls or while I was in your headquarters." That meant it was his fault Olly almost died. He'd led JB directly to them. Zac balled his hands into fists. *Stupid, Turner! You should have checked.* Obviously, JB was not only using them as a pawn in his game, but *they* were included in the list of players. Their lives were at stake. Zac stiffened at the thought of Olly's life on the line in this sick man's mind.

Sirens interrupted his increased anxiety, and he quickly checked the team's vehicles. His was the only one with a tracking device. He studied Olly's SUV. Snow intermixed with the embers as smoke rose upward. The storm had intensified. They needed to get on the road before it got worse. He walked back to the team. "Your vehicles are fine. Head to my station before the roads are impassable. My chief is expecting you."

"But will we be safe?" Lauren asked.

"I suggest you travel together. Safety in numbers." Zac would suggest a police escort, but he didn't trust anyone. "Take the back roads, but be careful. Call if you see any trouble. And don't talk to anyone about this case. JB has made it clear we're on our own here. If we involve anyone else other than our teams, he'll know. Plus, this action was a warning. We're also instruments in his game and need to be on alert at all times."

Lauren and Fraser nodded before heading to their vehicles.

Firetrucks, an ambulance and a police cruiser arrived at the scene. Firefighters jumped from their truck and extinguished the flames.

Two paramedics headed toward them.

Zac turned to Olly. "It's important they check for injuries."

She rubbed her temples. "I'm okay, Zac. Just a bit frazzled."

"I'd feel better if they look at you. Just to be sure."

"But—"

He raised his hand. "Please don't argue with me." He couldn't let her stubborn streak get in the way. "I'll speak to the officer while they examine you." He paused. "I'm sorry they used my cruiser to find us. I should have looked closer at my vehicle."

Her eyes softened. "Zac, you can't always be the hero. Sometimes things are out of your control." She tugged on his arm. "It's okay. We're fine. It's not your fault."

Even though her gloved hand rested on his arm, he remembered what her touch did to him. And those hazel eyes? They lured him in every time. *Step away, Zac.* "I'll be over there." He turned to Ziva. "Come."

His K-9 trotted by his side as they made their way over to the officer.

Thirty minutes later, Zac, Olly and Ziva were on their way to Stittsrock Falls. Zac had explained the situation to the officer as best as he could without revealing JB's game. Zac had told him the truth: he didn't know where the rocket-propelled grenade had been launched from or who'd fired it. Half-truth. It had to have been JB. Who else wanted them eliminated for disobeying?

The darkened skies had changed midafternoon day to dusk. The snow had intensified and now pelted the region. Even with his cruiser's wipers on full speed, they barely kept the windshield clear.

Zac leaned closer to get a better view of the road. "We may have to pull over and wait it out."

"Please, no. Grace is expecting me to pick her up soon. We have to get home." The worry in Olly's voice revealed her love for the foster child.

He stole a glance at the woman in his passenger seat. A wiry curl escaped her normally picture-perfect hair and dangled in front of her eyes. He resisted the urge to tuck it behind her ear and tightened his grip on the steering wheel, returning his focus to the slippery road. Zac prayed his Explorer's winter tires would continue to give him traction.

"We'll keep going, but if it gets worse, I need to keep you and Ziva safe." Zac looked into his rearview mirror, checking for any sign of a vehicle tailing them. So far, so good. "Tell me about Grace. Is she adapting to being in your home?"

Olly let out a prolonged sigh. "She is now, but it was tough at first. She'd just come from an abusive home. Coming from two parents who took their frustrations out on her to me. A single woman who didn't know what she was doing."

Zac caught the quiver in her voice. "You're so good with kids, though. I'm sure you won her over quickly."

"It took a bit of time for her to trust me. Trust that I wouldn't hit her." She paused. "Zac, to see that six-year-old with bruises—fresh and faded ones—broke my heart in two. How could anyone abuse a child?"

The anger in her voice revealed her love of children. His desire for a family surfaced. One with her, but he knew that would be impossible.

He would never put her or children at risk. Zac had kept tabs on his father. After British Columbia police had arrested Harry Burns for the murder of a rival gangster who had supposedly helped Zac's mother flee years ago, the crime boss had confessed his hatred for his wife and child. He'd spieled words in his interview of how he would one day get even with Zac's mother and take them both out, indicating he still searched for them after years of separation.

Zac would never put a wife and family in that type of situation. No, he would remain single—forever.

And it broke his heart.

He suppressed his frustration and concentrated on the drive back to their town. "I'm so sorry Grace went through that. I take it she's doing better now?"

"Yes, after some rough patches, we finally bonded. So much that I can't give her up." Once again, her voice hitched.

"Have you looked in to adopting Grace?"

"Do you think—?"

The tires hit a patch of ice, launching the vehicle into the path of an oncoming truck and stifling the rest of Olly's question.

"Hang on!" Zac yelled, turning the wheels into the skid. The tires caught traction and he swerved the cruiser back into their lane.

Zac's erratic heartbeat lessened with the threat over. "That was close. We—"

"Turner, what's your ETA?" Chief Bennett's voice boomed through his radio.

Zac pressed his button. "We're fifteen kilometers out, but the roads are bad. May take us a bit. Why?"

"JB just sent us another threatening letter. Time to get here. Now." He clicked off.

Zac's heart rate accelerated. Again.

Not only did they have to deal with a storm, but the Jingle Bell Bomber's relentless pursuit of some sort of justice for his cause.

Whatever that was.

Olive prayed for safety for the rest of the trip into Stittsrock Falls. The slippery roads played havoc and slowed their journey. The conversation had halted for the rest of their drive. News of another letter from JB had elevated her guard, and lots of questions filled her mind. She wanted to brainstorm with the team and review all documentation before providing a profile to the other officers.

Finally, after what seemed like an eternity, they arrived at Zac's station. Plows had cleared the streets and increased the size of their already huge snowbanks, obstructing their view. *Thank You, Lord, for keeping us safe.*

Zac parked beside a white SUV.

"Well, that was an interesting drive." Olive gestured toward the vehicle. "Good, Lauren and Fraser are here. That's her car."

"Awesome. We'll compare notes with my team. Let's go." Zac climbed out of his Explorer and went to the back. "Ziva, come."

Olive waited to see what the dog would do, her trepidation rising. Ziva jumped from the vehicle but remained at Zac's side. Clearly, the K-9 was well trained to stick close to her handler. Even though Olive was timid of dogs, she admired the beautiful chocolate Lab. Plus, she had saved Olive's life earlier. The irony wasn't lost on her. The object of her fears had protected her from harm.

Olive gathered her laptop bag and exited the vehicle, following Zac and Ziva into the building.

Twinkling Christmas lights adorned the small tree in the foyer while carols played softly in the background. She grimaced. It was a week before Christmas and she dreaded the season. She used to love this time of year, but ever since she'd miscarried and almost died on Christmas Day, she wished she could just sleep through the festivities.

However, her secret pregnancy from her college years during a time when God was far from her mind, had turned her love of Christmas into disdain. Even after many years, whenever December 25 approached, her body remembered the grief, and the pain bubbled to the surface. It was a time in her life she'd never shared with anyone—not even her sister, Scarlet.

Olive had gone overseas to spend Christmas

with her British roommate and that was when she'd discovered her pregnancy. Two days later, she'd ended up in the hospital and almost died after her miscarriage. Her shame of giving in to her boyfriend's pleas had silenced her from divulging why she now hated Christmas. Only her roommate knew the truth.

But this year she had Grace to think about. Olive wanted to give the little girl the best Christmas ever. She'd set aside her pain and put on a brave face. After all, don't parents always put their children first?

The experience of almost dying from her miscarriage instilled an unshakeable fear of getting pregnant again. The doctors had told her she was at high-risk of reoccurrence. She had vowed then to stay out of a serious relationship. But when Zac had asked her out, she'd felt a nudge from God telling her to let her fears go.

And look where that got you.

A broken heart.

Never again.

Olive stomped the snow from her boots as if sweeping away her former feelings for Zac, and followed him down the corridor.

An electrician fiddled with a light fixture and turned. "Oh, hey, guys. How are you?"

"Sebastian, buddy." Zac slapped the man on his back. "Glad you're here. I was going to call you.

So sorry, I have to cancel going to our hockey game."

"Oh?" The bearded thirtysomething was their town's favorite part-time electrician and could often be seen helping various companies. "Everything okay? I know how you don't like to miss them, along with Brett and Mitchell."

"Working an important case 24/7 right now."

"No worries, friend. We'll catch you next time." He tinkered with his tool belt.

"You remember Olive, right?" Zac asked.

"Of course." Sebastian held out his hand. "Good to see you again."

She shook his hand. "You too. I haven't seen you in ages."

"I know." His cell phone rang. "Gotta take this. Got another job to get to today. Zac, chat later?"

"You got it."

The man walked down the hall.

"I didn't realize you were friends," Olive said.

"Yeah, Brett and Mitchell brought him to a game a year ago, and we've continued going together." He pointed. "Let's head to consult with our team, shall we?"

Olive followed him into a room filled with computers, monitors, whiteboards and a long table. Other officers sat around it, chatting with Lauren and Fraser.

A slender man positioned at a whiteboard turned. "There you are. Welcome, Olive."

Zac instructed Ziva to stay in the corner and turned to Olive. "This is Chief Will Bennett. Have you met before? I know he's fairly new in our region."

Will held out his fist.

She pumped hers with his. "I haven't had the pleasure. Nice to meet you. Where did you move from?"

"Calgary. Welcome to our station. Glad to have you and your team here." Chief Bennett motioned toward the table. "This is Constable Ty Griffen."

The red-haired constable nodded. "Call me, Griff."

A burly man stood. "I'm Constable Pike. Head of the bomb unit."

"Nice to meet you," Olive said.

The chief pointed to a pretty blonde. "I believe you already know Constable Skye Lynch."

Skye gave Olive a quick hug. "Good to see you, friend. I'll be protecting Grace. Don't worry, she'll be safe under my care."

"I appreciate it, Skye." Olive placed her bag on the table and sat. "You're the perfect fit since you already know Grace."

"Yes. She trusts me, so that will be helpful. What are we going to tell her? Won't she wonder why we'll be living in a cabin for now…this close to Christmas?"

Olive withdrew her laptop and file from her bag, positioning them in front of her. "Good question."

Zac took the seat next to her. "Does she like Christmas?"

"Of course. What child doesn't?" It was just Olive who struggled with the season. "You should see her wish list." Olive sent up a silent prayer that a gift from the Jingle Bell Bomber would not be under their tree.

Chief Bennett tapped his pen. "What are you thinking, Turner?"

"We get a tree and decorations delivered to the cabin. Have a party decorating it. That would ease her mind." Zac fished out his notebook and pen.

"Great idea," Olive said. "She'd love that."

Will keyed his phone. "I'll get our admin, Brynn, working on the details. I'll send her to the cabin with everything and ensure it's fully stocked."

Lauren bounced in her chair. "This is going to be so much fun."

Zac raised a brow, tilting his head.

Olive could almost read his mind, and she agreed. Holed up in a cabin with strangers while hiding from a killer was not her idea of fun.

However, for Grace's sake, she'd muster up strength and put on a brave face. Anything for Ladybug—the nickname Olive had given her after Grace wanted a ladybug theme in her bedroom.

The chief cleared his throat. "Okay, let's get started as I know it's almost time for school to be dismissed and you'll have to pick up Grace." He walked back to the board and added Rick's picture. "Three victims so far. Our own Constable Jack Everett, Mary Jones, a letter carrier, and your coworker, Rick Vincent."

"A police officer, postal worker, and now a forensic investigator," Zac said. "I see a connection between Jack and Rick, but a postal worker?"

Olive opened the victims' files. "Plus, their ages vary—59, 51 and 34. Two males, one female. JB seems to pick randomly. Odd for a serial killer."

Fraser spread pictures out in the middle of the table. "The only commonality between them is his method. Pipe bomb in a Christmas gift."

"Don't forget the jingle bells," Lauren added.

Will wrote *jingle bells* beside *pipe bomb* on the board. "My question is…why did he target Olive and Zac for his supposed game?"

Olive bit her lip. "My theory is we both know him."

"Agreed," Zac said. "Sorry for keeping you in

the dark, Chief, but I had no choice. He threatened Olive's parents. I couldn't take that risk."

"But why did he plant two fake bombs and one real one in our building?" Fraser asked.

"He's taunting and testing us all in one." Olive fingered the note JB had written to her. "Chief, hand me the letter JB just sent to the office. How was it delivered?"

The chief passed her a piece of paper inside an evidence bag. "Courier. No return address."

Olive brought the typewritten message closer.

Zac and Olly,

I've only just begun. You see, there are still many naughty people on my list requiring one of my special gifts. Get some rest because the game continues tomorrow. And remember... I'm always watching...just like Santa.

Yours truly, JB

Olive inhaled sharply, her anxiety levels rising. A question haunted her.

How could they stop the Jingle Bell Bomber's deadly game?

FIVE

Zac analyzed Olly's ashen face as she waited for the teacher to bring Grace to the room. Her twisted expression proved to Zac that JB had rattled her normally solid demeanor. But who'd blame her? Obviously, JB targeted the two of them. Why, Zac couldn't figure out. Was it someone from their past? Or did JB just know them from living in a smaller town? Stittsrock Falls held a cozy community feeling among its residents. Neighbors looked after neighbors.

They had stopped by Olly's house and packed some belongings before heading to the school. Now, Ziva sat next to him, still on guard. The team trained her to detect explosives and search and rescue. Zac had worked hard to give the K-9 a dual role. Most police dogs were male, but Ziva was special. Not only was she extremely intelligent, but her strength had beat out other K-9 choices. Plus, it helped that she was lovable.

A petite, curly-haired brunette skipped into the

room, followed by her teacher. When the girl noticed Ziva, she squealed before rushing to their side.

Olly's earlier terror-stricken countenance transformed into pure joy, her love for the little girl radiating.

"Ladybug, I want you to meet someone." Olly pointed to him. "This is Constable Zac Turner and his K-9, Ziva." She turned to Zac. "Zac, this is Grace Patterson."

Zac squatted and held out his hand. "Hello, Miss Grace. Nice to meet you."

She timidly shook his hand. "Hi. Is this your doggie?"

"She's actually my partner."

The little girl's eyes widened. "Your what?"

Zac hesitated, thinking about how he could phrase what Ziva did on the force. He didn't want to scare Grace. "We work together. She helps me catch the bad guys."

Grace moved closer to Ziva and reached to touch her, but Olly pulled her back. "Ladybug, you can't pet her when she's working. That's very important."

"What does she do?"

Zac eased himself into a standing position. "Watch." He turned to Ziva. "Ziva, come." He walked to the door.

Ziva followed.

"Stay."

She obeyed and sat.

Zac walked out of the room into the hall.

The dog remained positioned.

"Ziva, come," Zac ordered.

She sprang to her feet and trotted to where Zac stood.

Grace giggled. "Cool!"

Zac returned to the room, Ziva at his side. "She helps me find things, too, but right now, we're all going on an adventure."

The six-year-old's jaw hung open and she turned to Olly. "Where?"

Olly tousled the girl's curls. "We're going to stay in a cabin in the woods. Zac and Ziva are coming too."

"But what about my toys?"

"I packed some for you. We're going to decorate another tree. Would you like that?"

Grace bounced on her tippy toes. "Yay! I love Christmas."

Once again, Olly's face contorted before quickly smiling.

What emotion went through her in that split second? Remorse? More importantly—why after Grace mentioned Christmas?

His cell phone buzzed, interrupting the questions running through his mind. He swiped the screen and read the text. "Olive, time to go. Brynn confirmed everything is ready."

"Let's go get your coat, Ladybug." Olly took her foster child's hand and left.

Fifteen minutes later, he drove his police Explorer down the long laneway, deep into the woods. His chief had picked this location for a reason. It was on the outskirts of Stittsrock Falls and hidden from prying eyes. The one thing the team required right now. Seclusion. Protection from the Jingle Bell Bomber.

Snow fell throughout the day and brought with it a fresh blanket. Christmas lights twinkled behind the white layer, giving off a beautiful display.

Zac had loved this time of year ever since he was a boy. It had continued into his adulthood and he enjoyed spending Christmas Day with his mother—even if their relationship had been strained after discovering the secret she'd kept from him.

"It's so pretty!" Grace shouted, pointing to the front of the cabin.

Brynn had outdone herself, and in record time. Garlands and lights had been strung across the veranda and entwined down each pole. *Pretty, indeed.*

"It is, Grace. Shall we go check it out?" Olly unbuckled her seat belt.

"Yes, Olly!" The girl waited for Olly to leave the vehicle and open her door.

Zac noted the girl's use of Olly's nickname and the fact that Olly hadn't flinched like she had when he'd used it. *Interesting.* Then again, he'd broken her heart.

And his with it.

Focus, Turner. Remember why you're here.

He shut the engine off and moved around back to let Ziva out. Zac noted all the other team members had assembled in the large ranch-style cabin. Thankfully, there was room for everyone.

Zac withdrew Grace and Olly's suitcases and followed them to the veranda.

The door flung open and Constable Lynch appeared, beckoning them forward. "Hi, Grace! Come in and check out the tree."

The girl bounded up the stairs and into the house.

Zac laughed out loud. "Well, she's certainly adjusting quickly."

"It helps that she knows Skye, as we have girls' movie nights often." Olly held the door open. "After you and Ziva."

She stepped back, distancing herself from the dog.

Zac prayed their close contact on this case and her interaction with Ziva would rid her of the fear consuming her. She had confessed when they'd dated that the scar the dog left on her face plagued her with the constant reminder of that horrific experience. He had kissed the tiny mark on the bridge of her nose and told her she was beautiful. However, she'd failed to believe him. *Lord, what would it take for Olly to put it behind her?*

Chili simmering in the slow cooker flipped him back to the moment, making his mouth water. He ignored the sudden hunger pang in his stomach and set down the suitcases. He stomped the snow from his boots, took off his jacket, and hung it on the coat hook.

Zac followed Olly and Grace into the living room area. The team sat next to the fire, in front of a gigantic bowl of popcorn, stringing it on a thread. Christmas ornaments, bows made of buffalo plaid, and red and green lights lined the long coffee table.

Grace squealed. "Can I help?"

Olly turned to Zac. "How did Brynn get all this ready and supper in such a short time period?"

"Perhaps elves helped her?" He chuckled. "How about we eat and then decorate after?"

"Sounds good."

Two hours later, after eating supper and decorating the tree, Olly sat reading a Bible story to Grace in the corner. Ziva snoozed on a doggie bed beside the fire. Brynn had thought of everything. Zac made a mental note to pick her up an extra Christmas gift.

The team had agreed that after Grace went to bed, they'd gather in the dining room to go over their game plan for tomorrow.

For now, Zac enjoyed listening to Olly's soft voice as she brought baby Jesus's story to life.

I could get used to this.

Zac dug his nails into the chair's armrests, extinguishing his emotions. *You know who you really are and you can't put her in that danger.*

He averted his gaze to the roaring fire to shift his focus back onto the case. Questions whirled through his mind. Who would JB target next? Could they find the bomb and stop it? Who was the Jingle Bell Bomber?

Shut your brain down. Time to unwind after a long and brutal day.

But how could he when a killer was on the loose?

Olive sipped her decaf peppermint-mocha-flavored coffee and stared at crime scene photos, specifically the pipe bombs left in JB's Christmas gifts. The team, including Ziva, had gathered in the dining room and set up a makeshift situation room. They agreed to keep the door closed and locked. They'd only eat in the kitchen. Olive didn't want Grace entering and seeing details about their case.

She brought the picture closer and studied the bomb. A tiny etching on the pipe's opposite end drew her eye. She picked up her tablet and flipped to the same photo, enhancing it. "Well, I'll be. I never noticed this before."

She turned her device toward Zac.

He leaned closer, his earthy scent wafting into her personal space.

Olive shot back in her chair. She had to distance herself from this man. His presence brought too much pain. Why had he really broken off their engagement? Lots of questions still tormented her. What had she done wrong? Was there someone else in his life? What if—

Stop it, Olive. Concentrate.

She focused on the picture and pointed to a black mark. "See there."

"'Dec 25.'" His gaze shifted to hers. "Is Christmas his end game?"

The other team members stirred and focused on their conversation.

Lauren got up and placed her hands on the back of Zac's chair, shifting close to him. "I want to see."

Olive kneaded the back of her neck as if rubbing away the irritation prickling at her from Lauren's brazen move. She suppressed her scowl and reached around her coworker, swiping the screen. "Let's check the other bombs."

Olive pointed. "There it is again." She reviewed

the other pictures and all had "Dec 25" etched on the device. "Okay, Fraser. Can you add to the signature column on the whiteboard that JB dates his bombs? The question is what happened on Christmas Day and is this his trigger?"

The blond analyst walked to the board and wrote the information beside the signature list. "Okay, so we know he puts his bombs in Christmas gifts and he signs each one. He also sends letters to the police and news media. That's his MO and signature. Anything else to add? Shall we build the profile?"

Olive raised her index finger. "Just a sec. Let's talk about possible motives first." She turned to Zac. "Thoughts?"

Zac tapped his thumb on his coffee cup. "What do we know from other serial bombers?"

Olive opened her laptop and clicked on her files, reading her notes. "Some motives are personal. Some are political. Sometimes the motive is revenge for being terminated after a workplace injury." She leaned back, folding her arms. "So, a wide variety."

Lauren typed on her computer. "JB's MO seems to be pipe bombs."

"Agreed. So far, anyway." Olive pointed. "Write that down, Fraser."

He wrote *personal*, *political*, *revenge* on the board.

Skye walked to the pine sideboard housing a coffee maker and a plate of gingerbread cookies. She filled her mug and snatched a treat. "So, which of these are his motive?"

Griff leaned forward in his chair, placing his elbows on the table and steepling his fingers. "Didn't one of his notes say something about 'naughty people' being on his list? Does he think he's Santa Claus?"

Olive chewed on a strand of hair, then dropped it. She had to break that unprofessional habit. "Let me see the note again. Zac, do you have it?"

Zac rummaged through a file and handed it to her, his fingers grazing hers.

She jerked at the jolt his touch sent and dropped the photocopy of the note. Their eyes held for a split second before she cleared her throat and picked up the paper. She reviewed JB's words, praying her face wasn't as red as her flushed cheeks felt. She couldn't let the others—or Zac—know how his presence awakened a flurry of emotions within her. "Okay, this leads me to believe JB's motive is revenge. He's out to get these naughty people."

Zac walked to the board and pointed to each victim. "So, he's been wronged by a police officer, forensic analyst, and a postal worker. That's a gamut of professions. Well, two are law enforcement related, but a postal worker?"

"Agreed," Griff said. "She doesn't fit with the others. What are we missing?"

"Let's do a more thorough background on our victims' personal lives. Dig deeper." Zac stuffed a cookie in his mouth.

Ziva yawned and stretched from her corner position before trotting over to her handler. Zac bent over and stroked the dog's head.

"Tell us about Constable Everett." Lauren picked up a file. "Says here he was married with three children. Wife deceased. Such a shame. What was he like as a cop?"

"Solid investigator," Zac said.

Griff winced but remained silent.

Olive sensed the officer struggled to offer more insight. "What is it, Griff? You don't agree?"

Griff eyed Zac. "I know you looked up to Jack, but he was rough around the edges. There were even rumors he was on the take."

Zac's expression hardened. "That's not true. Griff, you know Jack would never take a bribe. Someone started those rumors."

Skye fingered the heart dangling from her bracelet. "But how well did we really know him? Something happened to him after his wife died."

"When was this?" Fraser asked.

"A year ago. She was murdered." Zac returned to his seat, Ziva following. "Her case was never solved. I agree he was different after that. All of his kids were married and moved away. After his wife died, he was all alone. Wouldn't that affect you?"

The tone in Zac's voice surprised Olive. Clearly, the two of them had been close.

Griff drummed on the table. "He had financial troubles, Zac. Did you know that?"

Zac's eyes narrowed. "He made some bad investments, so what? Jack was not dirty."

The tension in the room tripled within seconds, silencing the team with an awkward break in the conversation.

Time to move on. Olive turned to Lauren. "You knew Rick better than I did. What can you tell us about him?"

"Divorced. No children. All around nice guy." Lauren's voice quivered.

Fraser changed seats and squeezed her hand. "Rick climbed up the ladder quickly and became leader of Forensics a year ago. He was good at his job. Church guy."

"Wait, church?" Skye asked.

Fraser nodded.

"Why question that, Skye?" Olive keyed more information into her notes on her laptop.

"Because Jack told me he recently found God."

"Okay. That's a connection." Olive popped out of her seat and wrote *church* under both Jack and Rick's names. She pointed to the female. "What about Mary Jones?"

"I remember reading about her. Just a sec." Zac sifted through the files until he found one and opened it. "Fifty-one, married, no children." He ran his finger down the page. "Here it is. Attended Stittsrock Falls Bible Chapel. Perhaps Jack went there too. I know Pastor Felix. Maybe we talk to him tomorrow?"

"Good idea." Olive closed her laptop and checked the wooden wall clock. "It's getting late, guys. We'll think clearer after a good night's rest." She picked up JB's letter to put it in the file folder. "Tomorrow we'll try—"

She gulped in an audible breath.

"What is it, Olive?" Zac asked.

She wiggled her fingers. "Give me the other notes."

Zac handed her the folder. "What do you see?"

Olive lined them up in front of her, examining each closely one by one.

She pointed to the *J* in "JB."

"Look how the bottom of the *J* is missing the edge of the loop in all of these."

Zac tilted his head. "So?"

"This tells me all of these letters were typed on a manual typewriter. The Jingle Bell Bomber is old school." A thought tumbled through her mind.

Was the serial bomber older than they'd originally thought?

SIX

Zac parked beside Constable Lynch's cruiser at Grace's school. Skye, Olly and Grace had traveled together, so Grace would feel secure.

After a restless sleep, Zac had slipped out of bed early. His mind had played tricks on him with noises throughout the night, but after he searched and came up empty, he went back to bed. Perhaps after their group session and discovery of JB being old school, he was on edge. He'd racked his brain trying to figure out the bomber's identity, and if he was truly someone from Zac's past. No one he knew fit the profile— or the partial profile. Zac had prepared breakfast for the team. He loved to cook, as it helped him unwind and think.

Zac had led Ziva around all their vehicles earlier, probing for bombs, but his K-9 had detected nothing. That told him that JB was unaware of their location.

Or the bomber had let them live…for now.

Zac cast aside thoughts of JB, got out of his vehicle, and walked around to release Ziva. He had assured Olly his partner would do a thorough search of the school and premises before the children arrived.

He walked to Lynch's vehicle and tapped on the window.

She hit the button. "You set to do your search?"

Zac leaned closer and peered at Olly.

She sat in the passenger seat, chewing on her hair.

A habit he once thought was adorable, but now only brought back painful memories. "Yes. You called the principal, right, Olive?"

"I did. She's here now. I see her car in the parking lot." She turned to look at Grace. "Ladybug, we're going to wait here for a bit, okay?"

"Why?" the little girl asked.

"Ziva needs to play a game and search the building first, okay?" Zac said.

Grace's eyes brightened. "Fun! Can I play?"

"Not this time," Olly said. "Maybe later you can play with her in the snow at the cabin."

The girl squealed and clapped. "Yippee!"

Zac chuckled at the six-year-old's enthusiasm. "Okay, we'll be back. Sit tight." He rapped on the vehicle's window frame before addressing Ziva.

"Come."

The two of them scoured the perimeter and

Ziva sniffed through the bushes but didn't alert to any explosives. Ten minutes later, he opened the front door and led his K-9 partner into the school.

The principal and janitor stood farther down the hallway and, from the appearance of Miss Bell's flailing arms, they were in a heated discussion. He hated to interrupt, but he and Ziva needed to conduct the search.

"Morning," he said loudly.

They turned at his approach. The janitor scowled but whistled "Jingle Bells" as he sauntered down the corridor.

Odd choice of Christmas songs.

Miss Bell held out her hand. "Welcome, Constable Turner. Sorry about Brad. It annoyed him you were conducting a search. Don't mind him. He takes pride in a well-kept school and assured me the premises were safe."

Zac shook her hand. "What's his name and how long has he worked here?"

"Bradley Longy. Thirty years, like me. Time for both of us to retire." Miss Bell paused, biting her lip. "He's been quite agitated and secretive lately, spending most of his time in his basement office."

Interesting. Zac dug out his notebook and pen, adding Bradley Longy to his list of suspects. Not that hibernating in the school's lower level qualified, but his evasiveness piqued Zac's interest.

"Thanks for the information. Ziva and I will start our search. We need to ensure the building is safe."

"Can you tell me why? Does it have anything to do with the Jingle Bell Bomber I keep hearing about in the news?"

"I really can't say, but I will have officers patrol the school frequently and Constable Lynch will be with Grace Patterson at all times." Zac stuffed his notebook back into his pocket and fished out a business card.

Her eyes widened. "Oh, dear. Is Grace in danger?"

"It's just a precaution." He handed her the card. "Please contact me if you see anything suspicious in your building."

"You mean like a wrapped Christmas present."

His muscles turned rigid. *Wait! They hadn't released that information to the public.* How did the woman know? "Why would you say that?"

"Just a guess. Why else would the bomber call himself the Jingle Bell Bomber?"

She had a point, but he still mentally added her to his list. Could JB be a woman?

He tucked the information away. "Gotta get to work. You have a good day." He tipped his hat at her before turning to his K-9 and releasing her leash. "Ziva, seek." The dog sprang into action.

He followed Ziva into a classroom. She spent

the next fifteen minutes sniffing through the small public school rooms, but failed to alert at anything suspicious. Thankfully.

Zac informed Miss Bell the school was safe before leaving the building with Ziva. He returned to Lynch's vehicle just as other students arrived.

He opened Olly's door. "We're good. Ziva didn't find a...a Christmas gift." He almost said "bomb," but remembered the little girl in the backseat with the big ears. Even though she gave off a shy vibe, Zac could tell she listened intently and he wouldn't scare her by using the wrong word.

"Time for school, Ladybug." Olly climbed out of the vehicle.

Zac opened Grace's door and unbuckled her seat belt.

Grace exited the cruiser. "Can Ziva come too?"

Zac knelt in front of Grace. "I'm afraid not. She has to work."

"You mean play more games?"

Smart girl.

Zac nodded. "But remember, you can play together later. Okay?"

"Yay!"

Olly placed Grace's backpack on the little girl's shoulders. "Skye will be with you today."

"Is she going to help me with my math?" The girl pouted. "I hate math."

Lynch tousled the pom-pom on Grace's hat. "Me, too, pumpkin." She held out her hand. "Let's go have some fun."

Five minutes later, Olly slid into Zac's heated cruiser. "All set. Skye was a big hit with the kids, but not so much with the parents. Even though she wasn't in uniform, they were still suspicious, as they realize she's a police officer. I took them aside and explained she was there as a precaution, but I'm sure they'll figure it out."

"I want to tell you about my conversation with Miss Bell." He explained what happened with Brad and also that the principal had somehow known about the armed Christmas gifts.

Olly huffed in a sharp breath. "But we kept that from the media."

"I know. Something was definitely off with both her and the janitor. In your expert opinion, do you think JB could be a woman?"

"I doubt it. Most serial killers are male."

"But it's possible?"

"Anything is possible. We can't rule—"

Zac's radio crackled.

"All units, explosion at Stittsrock Falls Bible Chapel on Third Street," Dispatch said. "Firefighters are en route."

Zac flicked on his siren and lights. "That's where we were heading today. Coincidence?"

"Highly unlikely." Olly banged the dash. "Let's go."

Zac's tires swerved on the icy parking lot as he turned onto the road, speeding toward the church with a question in mind.

Was this explosion part of the Jingle Bell Bomber's deadly game?

Olive stepped out of Zac's cruiser and wrapped her scarf closer to her neck. The frigid temperatures had been relentless since mid-November. Seems winter had arrived earlier than normal in their region, freezing everything in its path. Firetrucks, police cruisers and an ambulance had gathered at the tiny church. Flames shot out from the top of the building, embers and smoke drifting into the clear blue sky. Questions filled her mind. Was this somehow related to their case or just a coincidence? Dispatch had mentioned an explosion, but they didn't know what had caused it. If this was JB's work, why bomb a church? She prayed the building had been vacant when the blast hit.

Constable Griffen spoke to a firefighter while others fought to bring the fire under control.

Zac exited the vehicle and stood beside her. "I would tell you to stay behind, but I know your stubborn streak."

She dug her gloved fingers into her palms.

"You got that right. I realize the investigation portion of the case is not part of my job description, but I want to examine the scene. It may help with our profile. It needs to be solid."

"You think this explosion is tied to the case?"

"Don't you? At least one of our victims attended this church."

"True." Zac placed his hand on her shoulder. "Plus, I'd feel better with you close by for protection since it's obvious JB has targeted you."

She ignored his comment and gazed at a middle-aged man standing off to the side. "Is that the pastor?" Olive attended a larger church on the other side of town and wasn't familiar with this congregation.

"Yes. Let's start our investigation with him. Stay close." Zac walked to the back of the vehicle and let his partner out.

Olive followed the pair from a distance. Even though Ziva's presence gave her a sense of peace, her fears still niggled at her. *Give it to God.* It had been a phrase her mother had often said to her. Evelyn Wells had since succumbed to Alzheimer's and lived in a nursing home where she barely recognized her husband after years of marriage. *Mom, I miss you.* Olive longed to have a good, in-depth conversation with her mother, like they'd done in the past. She had been her sounding board on many occasions.

Olive set aside thoughts of her mother as they approached the pastor.

"Good morning, Pastor Felix," Zac said. "Are you okay?"

The slender, tiny man turned. "Oh, hey, Zac. I'm fine, just perplexed why someone would destroy this sanctuary."

"How do you know it was deliberate? Could it have been a gas leak or something?" Olive asked.

The pastor blinked rapidly. "You are?"

"Sorry, Pastor. This is Olive Wells." Zac petted his dog. "And of course, you remember Ziva."

She barked but stayed at Zac's side.

"Nice to meet you, Olive." Pastor Felix fished a bag from his pocket and held it up. "Because of this."

A blasting cap.

He handed it to Zac. "I waited for you to arrive. I knew with your bomb experience, you'd be here. Is this somehow related to the serial bomber in the news?"

Zac examined the device. "Felix, we can't discuss an ongoing case. I appreciate you preserving the evidence."

"You know my army background. I recognized it was important. I wore gloves when I picked it up."

Zac tucked the bag into his jacket pocket. "Tell us what happened. Exactly."

A firefighter yelled at another for more slack in the hose as they continued to fight the blaze. Two paramedics attended to a young woman at the back of the ambulance.

"Who's she, Pastor?" Olive asked, interrupting Zac's question.

"Church secretary. She was the only other person in the building at the time of the explosion." The man wrung his gloved hands together. "We were discussing my schedule for the day when we heard the doorbell and then the front door open and close. We thought it was our morning newspaper delivery. Klara left to check it out and that's when the explosion happened. I ran through the church and found her laying in the aisle and the place on fire."

A question entered her mind. "How far away were you from the blast?"

"Still in my office at the back of the church."

Far enough away to stay unscathed. Suspicion prickled as a knot formed in Olive's stomach, turning her breakfast into a hardened ball. She caught Zac's gaze and tilted her head, hoping he'd get her subtle question of whether this man could be trusted.

Back when they were engaged, they'd gotten so close, they'd finished each other's sentences. However, time had passed and there remained an unavoidable canyon between the two. Would he read her distrust in this man's story?

"Where did you find the blasting cap?" Zac asked.

"In the middle of the sanctuary aisle, several feet from the foyer." The man rubbed the bridge of his nose. "Why was my church targeted by the Jingle Bell Bomber?"

Zac squeezed the pastor's shoulder. "Let's not jump to conclusions. We don't know that for sure."

Good question, but why take the leap that it was JB? Could it have been an unhappy parishioner? Doubtful. Even Olive didn't believe that. After all, they'd been planning to come to talk to him today. Wait! Terror strangled her, sending her pulse zinging. Had JB somehow found that out and wanted to silence the man?

She thought back to their profile. "Pastor Felix, can you tell me if Jack Everett attended your church?"

The man's eyes clouded. "He did. His death saddened me. He was a troubled soul."

"How so?" Zac asked.

"Always questioning the ways of God. Speaking out with questions of sovereignty, why God allowed evil in the world. That sort of thing."

All good questions, but one remained. Why would that put the police officer on JB's list?

"Zac, buddy!" A firefighter walked toward them.

Zac turned and waved before addressing the minister. "Pastor Felix, thanks for your time. We may have more questions later." He pointed to the ambulance. "Please get checked out by paramedic Brett. He'll take good care of you."

The man nodded and headed toward the medical team.

The firefighter held a charred item. "Found this in the wreckage."

"Olive, do you remember Mitchell Booth? Firefighter extraordinaire?" Zac asked.

"Funny guy," Mitchell said, extending his gloved hand in Olive's direction. "Good to see you again."

She shook his hand. "You, too, Mitchell. I talked to one of your coworkers the other day. He told me you're moving."

"Yes, a great opportunity came up in Alberta near my hometown." He turned to Zac. "And you know how much I love the mountains."

"It's a perfect job for you, Mitchell. I'm just gonna miss you. Our hockey nights won't be the same." Zac ruffled Ziva's ears. "Ziva here will miss your treats."

Olive noticed the item in the firefighter's hand. "You found a gas can?"

"Yes." He held the jerrican up. "In the church's foyer. This is the point of the explosion's origin."

Zac's jaw dropped before he turned to Olive. "This can't be JB's work. Why would he change his MO?"

"Good question. Doesn't sound like this was part of his game." Olive stared at the pastor next to the ambulance as a question rose. Was he telling them the entire story?

Ziva growled, alerting them to danger.

"What is it, girl?" Zac asked, reaching for his sidearm.

Seconds later, a gunshot boomed.

Pastor Felix dropped to the ground.

The bullet silenced him from answering her unspoken questions.

SEVEN

Another shot rang out, intensifying Zac's alarm and stealing his air. He beelined toward Olly and shoved her behind his cruiser. "Ziva, cover!" His K-9 followed and secured herself into a down position like she'd been taught to do during gunfire. Zac raised his weapon, sheltering them. He stole a look to see where Mitchell had gone, but he was nowhere in sight. Zac silently prayed for his friend and the emergency response members. He held his breath and waited for more shots.

"Zac, you guys okay?" Griff yelled from a position somewhere around the firetrucks.

"We're good. Where's Mitchell? Brett?" Zac poked his head up, positioning his gun hand on the hood.

"Brett's in the back of the ambulance with the secretary," his fellow officer said.

"I'm behind Griff's cruiser. Help me." Mitchell's weakened voice revealed angst.

Zac's mouth dried within seconds. His friend

was in trouble and he needed to get to him quickly. He glanced at Griff's vehicle a few yards away. He turned to Olly. "I have to get to Mitchell. I think he's hurt."

"Go! I'll be fine." She gazed at Ziva, her face contorting.

Olly was anything but fine, but Zac would trust in his partner to keep her safe. "Ziva, stay." He also wouldn't risk his dog getting shot. She was too valuable to the team, especially in the deadly Jingle Bell Bomber case.

Once again, he peeked at the area, looking for suspects. Gunfire paused. Perhaps the shooter had fled. *Lord, keep us safe. Help Mitchell be okay.*

"Griff, cover me. I'm checking on Mitchell."

"Got your six," Griff said.

Zac inhaled, mustered courage, and bolted for Griff's car.

Thankfully, no shots came, and he scrambled behind the vehicle. Mitchell leaned against the tire, holding his arm and gasping.

"Mitchell! You're hit." Zac holstered his weapon. "Let me look."

The firefighter brought his arm down.

Zac unzipped his friend's gear. Blood soaked his clothes. "We need to get you over to Brett. You okay to walk?"

Mitchell nodded.

Zac wrapped his arm around his friend. "Griff,

cover us again. Brett, Mitchell's been shot. We're coming your way."

They crouch-walked to the ambulance as Brett jumped down from the back.

"Bring him over here," Brett said, motioning to the older paramedic to join him. "Leonard, get the gurney."

His partner headed back to the vehicle.

"Let me see," Brett said, examining the wound. "We have to stop the bleeding and get you to the hospital, but you'll be fine, my friend."

Zac let out the breath he hadn't realized he'd held. *Lord, please make Brett be right.* Both friends had been there for him during his and Olly's breakup. Even though Zac hated the fact they didn't know the real reason, he appreciated their friendship.

Zac noted the secretary cowering behind the ambulance. He'd like to hear her side of Felix's story to compare notes. Zac had read Olly's face and surmised she'd doubted the pastor.

"Mitchell, praying for you." Zac slapped Brett's back. "Take good care of him."

"You got it, buddy."

Confident the sniper had retreated as ten minutes had passed without further shots, Zac rushed over to Olly and Ziva. "You okay?"

She nodded. "Are we safe now?"

"I believe so, but I'm going to take Ziva and

do a sweep of the area just to be sure. Can you speak with the church secretary? I'd like you to check her story on what happened."

Her hazel eyes widened. "You suspected the pastor too?"

"Well, his story just seemed a bit too convenient. There has to be a reason JB killed him."

Griff approached. "How do you know it was JB? The MO is off."

"Who else would it be? We were planning on coming here today and the place is attacked? Then the pastor's taken out?" Zac took off his hat and scratched his head. "Sure sounds fishy to me."

"Good point." Griff gestured at the church. "I've called in Forensics, but not sure we'll find anything in the wreckage. Perhaps that's what JB wanted."

"I'm going to take Ziva and scour the perimeter. Olive will talk to the church secretary."

"Okay, I'll consult with the other firefighters." Griff walked back toward the smoldering building.

Zac squeezed Olly's arm. "We'll be back soon." He ignored what her presence did to him and turned to his partner. "Ziva, come."

Fifteen minutes later, he directed the forensics team to where he'd found the shooter's lair. Ziva had discovered the vantage point, but the suspect had fled. Zac had studied the area, noting that whoever had taken the shot had held the perfect view of the church's parking lot. They'd been fully exposed. The thought of something happening to either Olly or Ziva sent his heart racing.

The only piece of evidence he'd found was a shell casing. Hopefully, the team would find prints on it, but somehow Zac doubted the suspect would be so careless as to leave traces behind.

Zac also had enlisted the help of other officers to canvass the neighborhood around the church. He hoped someone had seen something.

Right now, Griff was trying to contain the growing crowd and media presence. Zac caught sight of a female reporter doing a live interview at the edge of the church property. Not good.

"Zac, got a second?" Olly headed toward him, holding her tablet in the air.

"Of course," he said. "What's going on?"

"JB just posted on social media, bragging about bombing the church."

"I bet he's watching this reporter right now." He pointed to the woman. "But wait, since when did he post on the world-wide web? I thought he was old school."

"I know of some older ladies in my church who are very active online, so it's possible." Olly swiped her screen. "Check this out."

He leaned closer and read the post on a popular platform, under the handle Jingle Bell Bomber.

No one is safe from my naughty list. Olly and Zac, sorry for changing my MO. I had to act fast as you were getting too close.

"Now he's targeting churches." He observed the young secretary standing near a firetruck. "What did you get out of her?"

"She's devastated at the loss of both the church and Pastor Felix. She spoke highly of him. However, she confided in me she was concerned about him lately." Olly peered at her tablet. "In her words, 'Pastor Felix wasn't himself.' Apparently, he'd been lashing out at people too easily, and that wasn't like him. Ever since both Jack and Mary were killed."

"But that's not abnormal. A pastor grieves the loss of church members. There has to be more to it." Zac studied the rubble left from the explosion. "Maybe we'll find something in this pile, but it's doubtful."

"We can always hope." She stuffed her tablet back into her bag.

Zac removed his notebook and pen. "I'm going to make a note to have the team do a deep dive on this church and its parishioners. Maybe something will stand out to us."

"Sounds good."

"Constable Turner," an officer ran toward them. "I have news."

Zac didn't recognize the young man, but his chief had enlisted officers from other nearby towns to assist with the investigation. They needed all the help they could get. "You are?"

"Constable Preston from two towns over. Listen, my sergeant sent me here to check with residents near the church bombing." He held up his notebook. "I found one sweet older lady who remembers seeing a white pickup truck every morning for the past week."

"Why is that unusual?" Zac asked. "Could be someone visiting a neighbor or something."

"True, but here's the odd part. The man stayed in his truck the entire time and when she went to talk to him—brave old soul—he took off. She also noticed jingle bells hanging from the rearview mirror. Plus multiple gas cans in the back."

Olly drew in a sharp breath. "When did she go out to talk to the man?"

"This morning," the young officer said.

"Did she provide a description?" Zac asked.

"Only that he wore a tuque and sunglasses." Constable Preston checked his notes. "Oh, and she took down the license plate number."

Smart lady. This could be a break in the case.

Zac scanned what was left of the demolished church building.

Had there been something linking the congregation to JB's deadly game?

Olive stared at the blank board they'd labeled "Profile" at the police station and balled her hands into fists. They had returned from the church scene with more questions than answers and her mind had blanked when composing the Jingle Bell Bomber's profile. *This shouldn't be so hard. You've done this before.* But this time, those she knew and loved were at stake. She *must* get every detail correct to protect the Stittsrock Falls community.

She had checked on Grace to ensure she was okay, and Skye had reported everything was fine at the school. *Lord, keep Ladybug safe.* Olive had fallen fast for the little girl and prayed she could keep her. She'd looked into adopting, but hadn't heard from her lawyer yet.

Olive eyed the decorations adorning the room and rubbed her stomach. An automatic reaction this time of year. However, this Christmas season, things were different. Grace was bringing Olive's joy back every day closer to the twenty-fifth. She squared her shoulders, determination setting in. They *would* find JB and solve this case before then.

She pushed her focus back onto the board, tapping the marker on her chin.

"You're in deep thought," Zac whispered, placing his hand at the small of her back.

She jolted.

"Sorry, didn't mean to scare you."

How could she tell him it wasn't that he scared her, but that his touch sparked memories of him, their inseparable relationship, and that he was the one who'd gotten away? Well, he'd walked away—his choice.

She smothered a sigh and turned.

And stared into his chocolate-brown eyes. He had crept up behind her and stood close. Too close.

Their gazes held. She resisted the urge to caress his handsome face and staggered back. *Concentrate, Olly.*

She unclogged the emotion in her throat and pointed to the board. "I'm frustrated with getting JB's profile right. His—or her—actions have been unpredictable."

He rubbed her arm. "You'll get it. You're good at what you do."

She blinked away her earlier feelings for him. "What did you find out about the truck?"

"I ran the plates and discovered it's registered to a shell company. The chief is looking into it further. He wanted us to complete the profile.

He's set up a meeting at the library with all emergency services in our community and surrounding areas."

"Why the library?"

"We don't have a big enough room to accommodate all of emergency services personnel. The chief wants everyone in on this case to stop JB. Firefighters, paramedics, officers from nearby towns."

"Makes sense."

"Oh, and there were no prints found on the shell casing," Zac said.

"Figures." She studied the empty board. "Time to get it done, then." She joined the team at the table and sat. "Lauren, Fraser, time to finalize our profile. Lauren, you go first."

Her lips turned upward in a captivating smile and she winked at Zac. "You got it, boss."

Olive winced not only at her use of *boss* but her flirtatious manner toward Zac. Why did that bother her so much?

You know why.

Ignoring her stab of jealousy, she stood and moved back to the board. "Go ahead."

"Okay. Female, mid-forties, knows—"

"Wait, why mid-forties?" Fraser asked. "I was thinking more like mid-fifties."

Great, even my team can't agree on the profile.
She stole a peek at Zac.

His twisted expression proved he'd had the same thought.

Lauren flew out of her chair. "Fraser, you always contradict me."

He stood, placing his hands on the table, leaning forward. "Don't be a baby."

Olive raised her hands. "Whoa now. You're being unprofessional."

Griff chuckled. "Glad to see we're not the only ones who fight at times."

Zac walked behind his fellow constable. "Not helping, Griff."

"Sit, both of you," Olive said.

Her analyst team obeyed.

Lauren pouted.

Fraser sat, folding his arms.

The tension in the room escalated tenfold. Time to get it under control—and fast.

Why were they fighting suddenly? Olive guessed her sergeant had picked the duo as they played off each other's strengths. What had changed?

Wait—Fraser didn't like Lauren's flirting because he had a crush on her. That had to be it.

She turned to Lauren. "Explain to Fraser why you think mid-forties."

"Even though JB uses an old typewriter, she's active on social media." Lauren drummed her long, manicured nails.

"So is my grandmother," Fraser said.

Olive reflected back to what Zac had told her regarding both the principal and the janitor. They'd acted suspiciously, but it didn't add up. Plus, her research into serial bombers told her they were both wrong.

"Olive, you're thinking something different, aren't you?" Zac asked.

Was he reading her thoughts again?

"I am. You both have valid points, but history tells me JB is male." She viewed her team.

Lauren's taut face told Olive the woman hated to be contradicted, but it couldn't be helped. They had to get it right.

Fraser jerked back in his chair. "But—"

"Hear me out." She wrote *male* on the board and turned. "The words he uses in his letters tell me he's even younger. Perhaps early to mid-thirties. An older person would use more elegant language, even someone in their forties."

Fraser picked up the letter folder and opened it, studying the messages. Seconds later, he turned to Lauren. "She's right. I totally missed that."

"Me too." Lauren caught Olive's gaze. "No wonder Sergeant Alexander made you the lead on this."

Olive still doubted her assessment and her sergeant's faith in her abilities. However, she wouldn't let her lack of confidence show. Not here. Not now. Memories of one wrong profile clogged her mind. She had been firm that the unsub had been female, but it had turned out she'd been wrong and they hadn't discovered it until after the man had killed three more people. She'd vowed she'd never let it happen again.

The door opened and a female poked her head inside, drawing Olive away from her thoughts.

"Oh, sorry. Didn't realize you were still in here. How much longer will you be? The chief asked me to clean this room." The slender woman stepped inside.

Zac walked to the door. "Jacqueline, give us another hour, okay?"

"Sure. I'll head over to my next job and come back." She retreated into the hall, but left the door ajar.

Zac frowned. "Why would the chief ask her to clean now? Odd."

Olive poised the marker. "Let's move on. Time to wrap this up as the team meets soon."

Two hours later, Olive followed Zac and Ziva into Stittsrock Falls Public Library. The older stone Victorian building had been a spot she'd loved to visit as a young girl. She'd enjoyed wandering through the rooms with her friends, trying to find the rumored hidden passageways and secret compartments. At one point, the librarian had found them huddled in a corner after they'd gotten lost in a darkened area and couldn't find their way back. She'd scolded them and threatened to tell their parents. They'd never ventured off again.

Evelyn Wells had teased Olive every time she'd caught her with her nose in a Nancy Drew book. Her mother had introduced Olive to her favorite childhood sleuth and, even after years had passed, Nancy had quickly become Olive's fave too. She made a mental note to add a couple to Grace's list of gifts. Olive enjoyed reading to her before bed.

"What are you pondering?" Zac's breath tickled her neck.

Olive lurched sideways. She hadn't realized he and Ziva had crept up on her so quickly. "Just that I want to add a Nancy Drew book to Grace's presents."

"I'm sure you're looking forward to Christmas."

She looked away and chewed on a stray hair. *If you only knew the truth.*

He squeezed her shoulder. "What is it, Olly?"

She flinched and her eyes snapped back to his.

"Sorry, I forgot." He made the motion of zipping up his lips.

She exhaled. "It's okay. It's just harder to hear my nickname coming from you after our…"

"Our breakup."

"Yes." She gazed into his eyes. "You never really gave me a proper reason, Zac."

A shadow passed over his handsome face. "Olive, I couldn't—"

Loud voices interrupted their conversation, followed by a crash.

"That didn't sound good." Zac raced down the hall toward the commotion.

Olive followed and halted at the sight before them.

The cleaner, Jacqueline, lay on the floor with books piled on top of her.

Sebastian, the electrician, squatted beside her.

Zac shoved books away. "Buddy, what happened?"

"She accused me of cheating and shoved me into the bookcase." Sebastian turned to Jacqueline. "Babe, I'm faithful. You know that."

Her lip quivered and she peered at Zac. "I'm sorry. This is all my fault." She hustled to her feet. "I need to finish cleaning." She left the aisle as the librarian turned the corner.

"Don't you guys realize this is a library?" she said in hushed tones. "Sebastian, finish your job and leave. Constable, some of your team have assembled in the conference room down the hall."

Sebastian pushed himself up. "Sorry. I'll get out of your hair." He left.

Olive dashed forward. "Let me help clean up this mess. So sorry for—"

Lauren's scream pierced through the library as every light flicked off.

Leaving them in darkness in the old building.

Olive latched onto Zac, terror consuming her body.

Had JB tried to stop them from sharing the profile? A question haunted her mind.

Just how close was this serial bomber to the team?

EIGHT

Another scream boomed through the building, thrusting Zac's adrenaline into overdrive. He held Olly by the waist, his grip tightening with each of Lauren's cries. Clearly, she was in distress. "Olly, I need you to stay here so I can check on Lauren."

"I'm good," she whispered. "Just caught me by surprise. I'm coming with you."

Knowing it would do no good to argue, Zac unsnapped his flashlight from his belt and turned it on before taking out his Glock. "Stay behind me. Ziva, come."

They hustled toward the commotion.

Footfalls behind him echoed in the darkness.

Zac shoved Olly to the side and pivoted, raising his weapon and light simultaneously. "Police!"

"Zac, it's me, Griff."

Zac expelled a hissing breath. "I thought you were in the room."

"No, got waylaid by the chief. What's going on?"

"About to find out." Zac turned back toward the doorway and entered the room. He shone the light.

Fraser lay on the floor, his mouth gaping open. Lauren huddled beside him, sobbing.

Olly squatted in front of Fraser, placing two fingers on his neck. She turned to Zac and shook her head. A tear glistened.

Someone had gotten to her team.

Zac studied the room. A firefighter hovered near Fraser's body while Constable Preston stood perfectly still in the corner. "Hey, man, you okay?" Zac holstered his gun.

Preston's eyes bulged as he snapped to attention. "My first day out of rookie school has been eventful."

Zac remembered those days well. His introduction to the force comprised of a high-speed chase and seeing a fellow officer gunned down. Not a great start. "I get it. The job can paralyze you. Can you tell me what happened?"

"We were all talking when those two analysts came in. They introduced themselves and Frazer stuffed a cookie into his mouth and took a few swigs of water from the water cooler. We were chatting for a bit when he complained of vertigo. Later he fell out of his chair, clutching his chest."

He pointed to Lauren. "That's when she started screaming. Then the lights went off."

"Buddy, what's going on?" Brett asked and hurried to Fraser's body.

"Hey there. Not sure what happened. Possible heart attack."

"No!" Lauren yelled. "Fraser was in perfect health. He was just bragging about it."

Zac addressed the others. "Did anyone else eat anything?"

Preston nodded. "I had a cookie too."

"Me too," the firefighter said.

Zac eyed the cooler. "Anyone else drink the water?"

They shook their heads.

Griff walked over to it. "What are you thinking, Zac?"

"Poison. Get that bottle to Forensics ASAP and find out when it was delivered." He turned to Brett and leaned closer, keeping his voice low. "Can you contact the coroner? We can't move forward with our profile while Fraser's body is in the room."

"On it." The paramedic took out his cell phone. "Oh, Mitchell's surgery to remove the bullet went well. He's going to be fine."

"Thank the good Lord." Zac observed Olly's rueful face. Her tortured expression proved she cared for her coworkers. He approached. "Do you want to call it a day? This is a lot to take in."

She froze. "Zac, why didn't Ziva detect the poison?"

"She's not trained in that area. Explosives and SAR." Zac jerked to attention. "We must ensure the building is safe. Get the power back on and check for bombs."

Olly swayed, holding her tablet. "You think JB orchestrated this and has planted a bomb?"

"Anything's possible." He clapped. "Listen, we have to evacuate the building." He addressed Preston. "I need your help. Get everyone out and check with the librarian on the fuse box's location. Get the lights back on."

"On it." Preston turned on his flashlight and left.

Zac approached Ziva, who'd stayed by Lauren's side. Zac ruffled her ears. "Good girl. Time to work. Ziva, seek."

She sprinted from the room.

"Olive, help get everyone out. I'm with Ziva."

An hour later, after they had cleared the library for bombs and restored the power, the group sat in a different room—free of food and water. Griff had returned and said Forensic was testing the bottle's contents.

Right now, Olly stood at the front of the room getting ready to address the emergency services personnel.

He noted her hand shaking as she held her

tablet. Obviously, losing Fraser had unnerved her. Zac moved beside her. "You've got this," he whispered.

She drew her shoulders back and nodded, determination showing on her face.

Zac clapped to still the room. "Folks, I realize today has been hard. First the church explosion, and now the death of a comrade." He failed to stop the choke in his voice. He inhaled and exhaled slowly. "It's affected us all, but we must band together. We're a community."

He gestured toward Olly. "Most of you know Olive Wells, but may not know her profession. She's a criminal investigative analyst for our federal police and her team has developed a profile of the Jingle Bell Bomber. That's why you're here today. My chief, who is tending to other tasks at the moment, contacted all of your leaders. We need our first responders here and in surrounding towns to come together and stop this maniac." He paused. "And to do that, we require a profile. Olive, take it away."

Zac sat across from Lauren.

Olly smiled. "Thanks, Zac. I agree. This has been a tough day, but Fraser would want us to press forward. He was a good person, so let's honor his memory by catching this killer." She swiped her tablet and connected it to the monitor at the front of the room, projecting her notes onto the screen.

"My team and I have spent hours reviewing crime scene photos, letters he's sent to the media and police, social media posts, and his victims. Here's the profile we've developed.

"First, the Jingle Bell Bomber—or JB—is a male in his early to mid-thirties. He doesn't have many friends. Spends most of his time by himself."

"How do you know that?" Preston asked.

"He crafts his bombs carefully and takes time to etch jingle bells on each of them." She flipped to a pipe bomb picture. "This tells us he's meticulous. Takes his time. That's not someone who'd be out partying all night. He's too particular." She pointed. "Look at the craftsmanship in the bells."

"Plus, it shows he's highly organized," Lauren added.

"Agreed." She directed everyone back to the screen. "He's a skilled worker who works alone. This gives him more time to make his bombs."

"What about the victims?" a firefighter asked.

"Good question. His targets appear to be random, but we don't believe that to be the case." She displayed all the victims' pictures on the screen. "We have a police officer, a postal worker, and a lead forensic investigator. We're still working on linking them together."

"What about Fraser?" Preston leaned forward.

"Do you believe JB killed him, too, or was it really a heart attack?"

Lauren banged the table. "It was murder!"

"I agree," Zac said. "Too much of a coincidence to have been a medical reason. Our lab is testing the water."

"The librarian confirmed the water dispenser was delivered thirty minutes before we all arrived," Griff said. "I agree with your assessment. This is too suspicious to be a heart attack."

"But, was it JB that killed him?" the young cop asked again.

Zac wished he could give the officer a clearcut answer, but it was too soon. "We really aren't sure. It's not his MO, but as I said earlier, we can't rule anything out."

Olly once again tapped her tablet and displayed pictures. "Good segue. Let's talk about his MO. We've kept this out of the media. JB puts his pipe bombs in Christmas gifts. That's how he attacks. I know…sick that he uses a special time of year as his weapon."

"Do you feel there's a significance?" Griff asked.

"We do because he's also engraved 'Dec 25' on his bombs," Olly said. "Maybe something in his past happened during Christmas."

Her face twisted in an expression Zac found hard to read. Just as quickly as it came, it passed. *Odd.* She'd had the same look earlier. It left Zac with a question. Was there something about Christmas that haunted Olly? The sudden desire to know more punched him in the gut. Did she carry a secret as he did? One she'd never shared with him?

Zac tapped his pen. "Christmas can be a tough time for many people while for others it's their favorite holiday." He reviewed her face, but this time she stayed stoic.

The door burst open and his chief bounded into the room. "Sorry to interrupt, but I wanted to bring JB's latest letter to you since you're all together. It just arrived at the station." He held up the bagged note before placing it in front of Zac and Olly. "He's picked his next victim and we have little time to save him."

Zac examined the typed note before reading it out loud.

"Zac and Olly,

The next person on my naughty list calls himself a mobile doctor. I disagree. He failed to save the life of someone dear to me, and now it's time for him to retire. Early. His Christmas present is under a tree where all the other mobile doctors reside. At one o'clock, he'll take his last ride.

Yours truly, JB"

"What does that mean?" Lauren asked.

Brett stood up quickly, his chair clanging on the floor. "One of our paramedics calls himself a mobile doctor and is retiring January first."

Zac bolted upward. "We have to find him. Who is it?"

Ziva jumped up at the ready beside her handler. She always knew when to act by Zac's voice tone.

"Leonard Fisher," Brett said. "We worked the church explosion today. He's not here right now because our supervisor tasked him with a rookie paramedic for the rest of the day. He's out on the road."

Zac turned to Olly. "Do you think he means the paramedic station by where other mobile doctors reside?"

Olly shut down the presentation. "Could be, but it seems too easy to me. Wouldn't he make his game harder? Brett, do you have a Christmas tree at your station?"

"Yes. I gotta warn him." He dashed out of the room.

Zac looked at his watch then addressed Chief Bennett. "It's twelve thirty. We have thirty minutes. Get Pike's bomb unit and firetrucks over there now. Ziva, come."

Time to get across town, find the tainted Christmas present, and defuse the bomber's game.

*　*　*

Olive stayed inside Zac's cruiser at his command as he and Ziva approached the small paramedic station. He wanted to clear the area with Ziva first and wouldn't put her in danger. After getting in touch with Brett, Zac had requested everyone to evacuate the building. The cold weather prevented them from waiting outside, so they remained in their cars, ready to reenter once Ziva gave the all-clear. *Lord, keep Zac and Ziva safe. Help save Leonard. We need a win here.*

Griff sat in his cruiser next to theirs. Olive guessed Zac had tasked him close to keep her protected. Other officers scoured the property for anything suspicious-looking.

Olive inspected the message JB had delivered to the police station. He had used the same manual typewriter, confirming her earlier assessment. For some reason, the bomber preferred the older method but yet was active on social media—an odd combination. She reread the words *He failed to save the life of someone dear to me, and now it's time for him to retire.*

Whose life had Leonard not saved? Was this entire vendetta because someone in JB's life had died? It made little sense. Surely, the death of a loved one wouldn't cause a break of this magnitude.

There must be something she'd missed.

An idea sparked and she entered Leonard's name in the search bar, hoping for a hit. Maybe something had been recorded that might help. Seconds later, Leonard's social media accounts appeared, along with a newspaper article where he'd saved the mayor's life, but nothing else.

"Ugh!" She stuffed the tablet back into her bag and checked the time. Twelve forty-six. The proverbial clock was ticking. "Come on, Ziva. Find the bomb." Olive admitted the K-9 was growing on her. Fear still spiked, but it was slowly lessening.

A commotion caught her attention. Zac and Ziva exited the building with Brett.

Griff got out of his vehicle and approached the group.

Olive stepped from the Explorer. "What's going on?"

"There's no bomb in the building." Zac gave Ziva her ball. "She checked all the presents under the tree and every room. No alerts."

"What are we missing?" Griff asked.

Brett looked at his watch. "It's twelve forty-eight. We're running out of time, or was this just a ruse to get us here?"

Olive read the note again and stopped at the last sentence. *At one o'clock, he'll take his last ride.* She latched onto Brett's arm. "Where's Leonard right now?"

"What are you thinking?" Zac asked.

She read the line out loud. "He played us. The bomb isn't here. It's in Leonard's ambulance!"

Zac pounded on his leg. "I can't believe I missed that." He addressed Brett. "Call him and tell him to get out of the vehicle. Fast. What's his ambulance ID?"

Brett pulled out his cell phone and spieled off the number before calling his coworker.

Zac radioed Dispatch, giving instructions for all patrols to be on the lookout for Leonard's ambulance. Possible bomb in the vehicle.

"Come on, Leonard, pick up!" Brett's frantic voice revealed anxiety over his fellow paramedic.

Lord, help us find him. Olive held her breath.

Brett clicked off. "Voice mail. What do we do?"

Olive crossed her arms, trying to keep her body warm. "Find out from 9-1-1 where he went on his last call."

"Good thinking." Brett walked away, contacting his dispatcher for the information.

A lump formed in Olive's throat. Her mistake might cost Leonard his life. *Why, Lord, didn't You show me earlier?* She fisted her gloved hands. "I'm so sorry, Zac. I should have caught that." Her voice stammered.

He embraced her and rested his chin on the top of her head. "Not your fault. JB fooled us all."

The K-9 nudged Olive's leg as if offering her comfort too.

I could get used to this, even Ziva's presence. She tensed.

Zac broke your heart. Back away.

She couldn't go there. She separated from his hold. The simple hug awakened fresh pain.

Brett approached at a quickened pace. "Leonard was called out to the outskirts of Stittsrock Falls. The rookie paramedic is with him." He gave them the address.

"Let's go!" Zac sprinted toward the Explorer, shouting the location into his radio.

Ziva followed her partner at lightning speed.

Olive's breath hitched. Now they had two lives to save.

In less than ten minutes.

NINE

Zac accelerated, his Explorer skidding on the icy road. It took them three long minutes to get around the downtown traffic before heading to the home on the edge of Stittsrock Falls—ten minutes away. No way they'd make it in time. He banged the steering wheel. He shared Olly's remorse over not figuring out JB's subtle clue. *Stupid, Turner! You're not on your game.*

"It's not your fault either," Olly said. "We both should have figured it out. We were just in a hurry to save Leonard that we missed JB's tricky clue."

She's reading his mind again. He remembered her knack for it, she had done it frequently when they'd been together. He stole a peek at her.

Her softened expression revealed the kindness he loved. Her enormous heart had always impressed him. Even when others had mistreated her, she'd given them the benefit of the doubt.

Except for him.

But he knew it was for her own protection, so he took the blame. He would not let his father find out about Olive Wells.

Zac returned his eyes to the road and an idea formed. He took a hard right, swerving onto a side street. "Going to take the back roads. Less traffic should make up time."

At least, he prayed it would.

Eight minutes later, Zac turned down the street where Leonard and his partner had been dispatched. The ambulance sat in the driveway. Zac parked along the curb.

The shabby house appeared to be abandoned.

"Something is wrong here," Olly said. "There's no way someone is living in that rickety house."

"Agreed. This feels like a trap, but where is Leonard?"

His radio squawked.

"Constable Turner, be on alert," Dispatch said. "Nine-one-one call just received of a possible armed intruder in your area. Sending backup to you now."

His pulse ratcheted up, tensing his already tightened muscles. "Copy that." He turned to Olly. "Stay here. Ziva and I will check the ambulance." He paused. "Do you have a weapon?"

"No. I'm an analyst."

They had gone to the shooting range a few times, so he knew she could fire a weapon. Quite well. "One sec." He went to the rear of his cruiser and took out a backup Glock.

He returned to the front seat and handed it to her. "I need you to be safe. Do you remember how to use it?"

She fingered the weapon. "Of course."

"Good." He checked the time: 1:05. "The bomb hasn't gone off. Maybe JB was bluffing."

Olly straightened in her seat. "He's watching and waiting to set it off."

"Why do you think that?"

"A hunch. Please be careful."

He nodded and opened his K-9's door. "Come."

Ziva obeyed, but remained at his side.

Zac took a few steps toward the ambulance. "Ziva, seek."

She steered directly toward the vehicle and sat, confirming Zac's fear.

The vehicle was indeed armed.

He backed up onto the street, far enough to get out of a blast trajectory. "Ziva, come!" Zac wouldn't let the dog be caught near the ambulance, in case JB was observing and detonated the bomb.

She dashed back to his side.

Zac's cell phone buzzed, announcing a text. He fished it out and read the message.

I don't kill dogs.

An explosion lifted the ambulance's back end off the ground, sending a ball of fire into the air.

Zac dove into a snowbank, tugging Ziva with him.

Fear stole Zac's breath and he wheezed, struggling for air.

Beside him, Ziva whimpered.

Was she hurt? Zac mustered strength and breathed in and out multiple times, regulating his erratic heartbeat.

He had to protect his partner.

Olive struggled with her seat belt. Zac and Ziva were in trouble and needed her. *Lord, help them be okay.* Finally releasing the buckle, she scampered from the Explorer and ran toward them. "Zac! Ziva!" She gazed at the obliterated ambulance. No way anyone survived the explosion. She fell to the ground in front of the pair. "Please tell me you're okay."

Zac propped himself up on his elbow. "I'm fine. Ziva whimpered, so I was just checking her over." He turned to his K-9. "Ziva girl, you okay?" He hugged the dog.

Ziva barked and rose to her feet.

Olive petted the dog's head. "I guess that means yes?"

"Appears that way." He rubbed Ziva's ears and kissed the top of her head. "Good girl."

Olive pushed herself to her feet and stared at the engulfed ambulance. "Close call."

"Too close."

Olive stuffed her exposed hands into her pockets. In the rush, she'd forgotten her gloves in the vehicle. "How did we make it here before it went off?"

"JB waited for us."

"What makes you say that?"

Zac stood and held out his phone. "He texted me and knew Ziva was by the ambulance."

Her jaw dropped. "He's been watching. Where is he?" She pulled out the Glock.

Sirens sounded nearby.

"That'll be the bomb unit we called in earlier, and firetrucks," Zac said. "I'm going to check to see if anyone was inside." He nudged her behind the Explorer. "Don't move. I'll be right back. Ziva, stay."

The dog obeyed, nudging close to Olive.

Olive crouched and waited.

Zac shielded himself from the flames and peered inside the ambulance, then circled around to the other side before running back to his Explorer. "They're both deceased." His shoulders slumped.

"But why didn't they get out of the vehicle? Even to check if anyone was in the house?" It made little sense. "Plus, wouldn't they have heard our approach?"

Zac rubbed his chin. "They must have been drugged. That's the only thing I can guess."

A second ambulance parked haphazardly at the curb, and Brett jumped out. "Leonard!"

He raced toward his friend, but Zac yanked him back. "He's gone, Brett. I'm sorry."

"No!" Brett crumpled to the ground.

Olive moved beside Zac's best friend and brought him into an embrace. "I'm so sorry. It's hard to lose a coworker." Olive would know as she'd just lost two. Adrenaline kept her from succumbing to the pain of death, but she realized it would happen. It was only a matter of time.

The bomb unit and firetrucks parked close. Firefighters hopped from their truck, ready to fight their second fire of the day.

Lord, when will it end?

Brett drew away from her and stood, clearing his throat. "Sorry. Leonard taught me the ropes. We'd grown close over the years."

Zac squeezed his shoulder. "Don't apologize. We understand."

"Thanks, bud. I must call my boss." Brett wavered to his ambulance and climbed in.

"Will he be okay?" Olive asked.

"In time." His gaze held hers. "How about you? It's been a rough day, and it's not over yet."

"God gives me strength. You?"

He averted his gaze. "He used to, but I'm not so sure anymore."

What did that mean? Zac's faith had always been strong. Maybe she'd never really known him as well as she'd thought she had. After all, he'd broken her heart out of the blue and hadn't explained why.

He extracted his cell phone from the holder on his duty belt. "I'm going to get the chief to request the 9-1-1 call that brought Leonard here. Perhaps we can learn something from the caller's voice."

"Good idea."

Zac glanced down the street. "Would you speculate JB is still out there? What's your professional opinion?"

She shivered, not from the cold, but from a sudden wave of trepidation penetrating her body. Had her adrenaline finally failed her and she'd caved to the day's terror? She leaned against the Explorer to steady herself and nodded. "I'm guessing that his personality wouldn't allow him to walk away."

Heart palpitations incapacitated her and the sudden desire to hear Grace's voice rose. She inhaled and fished out her cell phone. "I want to check on Grace." She punched in Skye's number and walked to the back of the vehicle.

Her friend answered on the second ring. "What's up, Olive?"

"Wanted to make sure Grace was okay."

"She's fine." Skye chuckled. "She's one smart little girl. Answering the teacher's questions quickly and accurately."

Olive's shoulders loosened with relief. "She's fast becoming the teacher's pet." She checked the time on the screen. "Watch for a tail on your way to the cabin, okay? It's been a hard day and I want you and Grace safe."

"Understood. I'll see you soon. We'll be leaving in five minutes." Skye hung up.

Olive scanned the crime scene.

Firefighters had the flames under control while forensics studied the area intricately. Griff stood next to them, pointing at a piece of metal on the ground. The group would bag the evidence and report their findings.

Observing the team brought emotions back from the loss of Rick. He'd been the best of the best in their unit, catching details others had missed. He left a gaping vacancy in their department. Fraser's death turned the hole into a crater. How much more could her team take? She bit her lip, warding off a tear welling. She needed to get away from the violence. If only for an evening. Unwind. Pretend her topsy-turvy life was normal. She eyed Zac.

Right. Far from it.

She huffed and returned to where Zac spoke to the fire chief. "School will be out soon and I want to be back at the cabin when Skye and Grace return. Can we cut our day short? I think we've earned a reprieve."

As if this case would give them a time-out.

Zac shook the chief's hand. "Keep me updated." He guided Olive by the elbow back to the Explorer.

"Sorry for interrupting. I just wanted to get away from all this." She waved her arm in the scene's direction.

"I'll radio the chief and tell him we're heading to the cabin."

"Thank you." A snowflake floated onto her shoulder, followed by others. Clouds had snuck in without her realizing the skies had changed. "We best get going before we get another storm." The cabin was on the outskirts of town, but in the opposite direction.

"Ziva, come," Zac ordered.

The three of them hopped into the cruiser.

Five minutes later, Zac drove back onto the highway leading into town.

A flash of white caught Olive's eye and she looked in the passenger-side mirror.

A white pickup sped toward them at rapid speed, appearing out of nowhere and clearly intending to ram them.

"Zac, look out!" she yelled.

He stepped on the gas.

But not in time to avoid a rear-end collision.

The Explorer spun on the icy road and headed toward a steep embankment.

Olive clutched the grab handle on the top of her window, bracing for what was to come.

She shut her eyes and prayed for protection.

Zac struggled to maintain control of the Explorer and keep the tires on the road, but the icy conditions took over and sent them careening over the side. "Hold on!" *Lord, I know I haven't talked to You lately, but please protect Olly and Ziva.* The most important girls in his life. Grace now too. He gripped the wheel and held his breath as his vehicle slid down the embankment, nose first.

Seconds later, the Explorer crashed at the bottom. The airbags deployed as the windshield shattered. The impact stole his air and the sensation of being punched in the face hit him hard. He pushed the bag out of the way, gazing at Olly.

Her face rested in the airbag, her body stilled.

"Olly! Ziva!" His frantic voice boomed.

The dog barked. *Thank You, God.*

"Olly, wake up." Zac fumbled for his seat belt, but the locked mechanism wouldn't give.

He pushed the button harder, finally releasing its grip.

He hauled out his multi-tool and sliced into Olly's airbag. It deflated instantly. He leaned her back against the seat to help clear her airflow. He checked her pulse and breathing. Both steady. The impact had knocked her unconscious, but she was alive.

Ziva barked, alerting him to a second danger more disastrous than the first.

Gas.

His partner had smelled the leak before Zac.

He shot out of the vehicle and released Ziva from the back on his way around to Olly's side. The crash had cracked the window. He lifted the door handle, but it wouldn't budge.

No! Please, Lord.

He tried again.

Stuck. The impact must have jammed the locking mechanism.

A flame rose from the hood.

Zac had no choice. He had to break the cracked glass to save her life. There was no time to haul her out through his side.

Once again, Ziva barked. She sensed the pending danger about to erupt.

He unclipped his baton and rammed it into the window, praying the slivers wouldn't slice into Olly's face. Unlocking the door, he yanked it open and unbuckled her seat belt.

He tugged her from the vehicle and lifted her into his arms. "Ziva, come."

He trudged through the snow and up the embankment. He turned at a whooshing sound and stole a glimpse at the Explorer. The flames ignited the fuel and, seconds later, the gas tank exploded.

A car door slammed, bringing his gaze back to the road.

The white pickup had stopped, but the driver was nowhere to be seen.

Olly stirred in his arms. "I'm awake."

"You passed out from the impact."

"I can walk." She pushed away from his embrace.

He gently set her down.

Her knees buckled and she clung to him. "Just give me a minute."

A shot cut through the air, blasting snow from the bank beside him.

"We don't have a minute!" No way would they be able to outrun the shooter in the deep snow. Zac unholstered his weapon and shoved Olly behind him.

Ziva barked.

Zac looked in her direction and noticed the object of her cry.

An abandoned barn a few yards away. He pointed. "Can you make it that far?" He pulled on his radio to call in their location, but the impact must have severed the cord from the mouthpiece. He'd have to rely on his cell phone, but right now, they had to move.

Another shot propelled them forward.

"Ziva, come!" Zac latched onto Olly's hand and tugged her toward the building, keeping his weapon raised.

Praying all the way.

TEN

Olive's breath drew ragged with each step she took. She stumbled in the snow but caught her footing, relying heavily on Zac's support. Even though the barn was close, the distance seemed like miles. Her jelly legs grew weaker, but she willed them forward. *You can do this. You have to do this.* But losing consciousness had taken more out of her than she'd admit. The jolt of cold air had snapped her awake, but the throbbing in her head didn't help the situation. Why was JB shooting at them? What rule had they broken?

Snow and strong winds now hammered the region, dropping in heavy amounts that impeded their path. Plus, her gloves and everything else were back in the Explorer. How would they survive the bitter cold? *Lord, send help.*

At last, the barn came into view. However, its rickety condition offered no promise of a haven.

"Quick, get inside," Zac yelled over the brisk wind gusts. He tugged the double doors open.

Ziva bolted into the building and Olive followed.

Zac closed the doors, leaving them in darkness peppered with strands of light beaming through the cracks in the slotted wood planks.

"Zac, he can get to us in here. We're. Sitting. Ducks." Olive's words came out jagged.

Zac peered through a break in the boards. "I don't see anyone." He tugged his cell phone from his belt. "Ugh. No service. Yours?"

"It's in your cruiser. It fell to the floor when we went over the embankment. Try your radio."

Zac held out the severed cord. "Broken."

Great. They were trapped with no way to call for help. *Lord, what are You doing?*

Ziva rubbed against her legs, lingering by her side.

Could the dog sense her growing trepidation?

"Wait! My cruiser is equipped with GPS. That should help them locate us." Zac looked out the wood slit again. "The blinding snow might hide the suspect's approach. Stay alert." He shone his flashlight around the barn.

The beam revealed a rusted tractor and baler in the corner.

"Get behind the farm equipment. It will at least give us some type of cover." Zac flashed the light again. He holstered his gun, picked up a pitchfork, and slipped the wood portion through the barn door handles. "Hopefully, this will block the shooter's entrance."

She scrambled to the tractor and crouched behind the large, flattened wheel.

Zac squatted beside her, Ziva following.

"Do you think the barricade will hold?" she asked.

He nudged her back and placed himself in front of her. "Doubtful. A hard slam into the door would probably break it off its hinges."

His honesty refreshed her, but also scared her at the same time. "Let's pray your constables find us first."

She wrapped her arms closer around her body. The drafty building did little to keep out the arctic winds. "It's freezing in here."

Ziva inched closer to her. Once again, seeming to sense her mood.

The K-9's body temperature not only warmed her, but brought a wave of peace. Olive snuggled closer.

"See, Ziva wants to help you, not harm you."

Olive stroked the girl's belly. "She's a good one."

Zac moved closer. "She is. Not sure what I'd do without her. She's saved my department's necks many times by finding explosives."

"Take some credit. You've trained her well."

"I met her as a pup and knew right away I

wanted to be her handler." Zac reached over Olive and petted his dog's head.

Olive braced herself. Being this close to the man she'd fallen in love with brought feelings back she wanted to keep suppressed. Her heart wouldn't survive another devastating blow a second time.

"What are you thinking?" Zac asked.

How could she share her heart when they had to work together? It was already hard enough to be in his presence, but she wouldn't put the investigation at risk by adding conflict into the mix. Lives were at stake.

"Just trying to figure out how we're going to get out of this mess." Half-truth. "Grace and Skye should arrive at the cabin soon. I told Skye I'd be there. Now they'll worry."

Zac put his arms around her. "Let's not go there yet. Surely, Chief Bennett will discover our location and send help."

The wind howled, bringing with it a gust of chilly air through the holes in the barn walls.

Olive rubbed her arms. "It's freezing in here. Do you think the shooter is gone? Maybe we should start walking."

"Olly, it's colder outside than in here. Besides, I bet someone will see the smoke from our crash and call 9-1-1."

"I sure hope so, or we'll freeze to death."

He tightened his hold on her. "I won't let that happen to you."

Her body numbed. His powerful embrace had always been her undoing. The way his arms folded around her body comforted her and gave her a sense of peace, telling her everything would be okay.

Lord, I can't do this. It still hurts.

She recoiled from her crouched position against him. "Don't, Zac."

"I'm sorry," he said. "I just wanted to keep you warm and reassure you it's going to be okay."

"I can't take being this close to you. You broke my heart." She hated the quiver in her voice. It had been eighteen months. Why wasn't she over him?

"I realize that." He caressed her face before fingering her scarf. "I broke mine with it."

"Then why did you leave?" She paused. "And tell me the truth this time. What did I do wrong?"

Olive, why did you bring this up?

The words had spewed out before she could stop them. Too late to take them back now.

Zac took her hands in his. "It was never you."

She pulled away. "Don't give me that 'it's not you, it's me' nonsense. I don't buy it. You're not telling me everything."

Zac walked to the small window on the barn's opposite side and peeked out. "I just fell out of love. I'm sorry."

"I don't believe you. I've noticed a reconnection between us the past couple of days. Tell me I'm wrong and I won't bring it up again."

He turned. "You're my friend. That's all you'll ever be. I'm sorry if you've felt otherwise."

What? Had she imagined something that really wasn't there, or was he not telling her the truth?

One thing she knew for sure. She had to get out of the barn. Away from him.

She rushed forward, wrenched the pitchfork out, and tugged the door open.

Confronting a killer outside was easier than having to face the man inside the barn.

"Ziva, come!" Zac grimaced and barreled after Olly. *What have you done?* He hated that he'd just lied to her, but he couldn't tell her the truth—for her protection. His mother had begged him to let Olly know, but Zac hadn't been willing to risk her life.

But…he'd just done the one thing he'd wanted to avoid.

Put her in a killer's sights.

"Olly, wait!" He took out his weapon and followed her. However, the intense snowstorm obstructed his view—which direction had she gone? *Lord, no!* She wasn't dressed for this type of weather. Her hat and gloves were back in the car.

Ziva brushed up against his legs, reminding

him of her presence. She was an explosive detector dog, but he'd also trained her in search and rescue. Plus, his dog's nose was her superpower, but would she catch any of Olly's scent lingering on Zac's fingers from his touch of her face and scarf?

Zac bent down. "Girl, we have to help Olly. Smell my fingers." He held his hand under Ziva's nose, letting her catch a lengthy whiff and praying the long shot would work. Zac stood and put his gloves on. "Ziva, search!"

She barked and hurtled toward the road.

Zac struggled to keep up to the K-9. Had she caught wind of Olly's scent, or was she racing after something else? Either way, he needed to keep up with her.

"Olly, where are you?" he yelled.

Only the howling wind greeted him.

She couldn't have gone far in that short amount of time, but he also knew how a snowstorm could easily distort someone's perception of their surroundings. Zac followed Ziva through what he guessed was the field beside the barn. The deepened snow hampered their search. How many minutes had passed since Olly had run out of the barn? Five? Ten?

He offered another prayer for her safety.

If God even listened to him. Not that Zac blamed Him. Ever since he'd found out about his real identity, he'd struggled with God's sovereignty and how He could control every aspect of their lives.

Ziva's bark disrupted further thoughts of God. Had she found Olly? Zac searched to locate his partner, but she, too, had disappeared into the snowstorm while Zac had been deep in thought. Stupid.

"Where are you, girl? Olly!" The wind softened his cry.

Come on, Ziva. Show me where you are.

Voices drifted from the left—or so he assumed. His inward compass was now distorted, and he didn't trust his normal keen sense of direction.

Had the killer returned and brought reinforcements? Zac gripped his Glock tighter.

Once again, Ziva barked, giving Zac hope and direction. He turned toward the K-9's signal. "Ziva, again." He risked exposing their location, but had to yell to find them.

The dog barked.

Zac was close.

Minutes later, Ziva came into view. She sat beside a huddled form leaning against a tree.

"Olly!" Zac holstered his weapon and removed his gloves, putting them on her. "You're freezing."

"S—S-so-rr-y. Lo-ss-tt." Her stuttered words revealed her frozen state.

He brought her into his arms. "I'm sorry too. I've got you."

The voices intensified.

He stiffened. "Someone's coming." He freed his gun again and raised it in the direction.

"Zac! Olive! Ziva! Where are you?"

Griff arrived.

Zac's taut shoulders released. *Thank You, God.* "Over here!"

Ziva barked, helping to give them their location.

Seconds later, Griff and Zac's chief appeared through the snowstorm.

"There you are," the chief said, approaching them quickly. "You okay?"

"Olive needs a paramedic." Zac brought them both to their feet. "Did you find the shooter? The white pickup rammed us over the embankment, then he started shooting."

"No pickup in sight, but I'll call it in," Griff said. "Ambulance is on the way."

"How did you find us?" Zac asked.

"Nine-one-one call. Someone saw the smoke from your accident and investigated. They noticed it was a police vehicle." Chief Bennett took off his hat and put it on Olly. "This should help."

"Thank you." Olly's voice still wavered.

The chief yanked up his hood. "I tracked your GPS but couldn't find you when we arrived."

"We took cover in a barn because of the shooter, and then got separated." Zac left out the rest of the story. That was for his and Olly's ears only.

Chief Bennett grabbed Olly's arm. "Let's get you to my Explorer before the ambulance arrives." He turned to Zac. "Should you get Ziva checked too?"

"Absolutely." Zac wouldn't risk not getting her examined, especially after the bombing, accident, and being out in the cold.

Zac followed the group to the chief's vehicle with one question tumbling through his mind.

Had he put the investigation at risk by ruining his and Olly's working relationship?

Olive nursed a cup of steaming hot chocolate, trying to warm up from her foolish trek out of the barn and into the blinding snowstorm. She blamed herself for putting both Zac and Ziva at risk. She should never have brought up the subject of their breakup or left the barn's shaky protection. Still chilled to the bone, even after hours of sitting beside the cabin's roaring fire, she hoped the beverage would help.

Zac had insisted the paramedic check her out and after Brett had cleared her, they'd picked up another police cruiser, a new cell phone and tablet for her before heading to the vet. Ziva had passed without any issues. Seemed the dog was in better shape than she was.

Grace and Skye had been happy to see them after waiting frantically for word on their whereabouts. The group had ordered pizza for supper, but after the day's events, Olive's appetite had wavered and vanished after a couple of bites when the food hardened in her stomach.

Lauren had secluded herself in her room, claiming a headache, but Olive knew the truth. She struggled with Fraser's death. Olive too. Griff and Skye had also retreated to their rooms. It had been a long day for everyone. After reading to Grace and putting her to bed, Olive sat beside the fire with a notepad, trying to remember everything in her tablet notes left in Zac's demolished cruiser. She let out a seething sigh.

"What is it, Olive?" Zac walked into the room and grasped the poker stick from the holder before stirring the coals to create more heat.

She registered his use of her full name and not her nickname. He was still upset. Not that she blamed him.

"Trying to remember my notes lost in the Explorer's fire. I was able to get into our system to retrieve my files, but I had made additional comments using an app on my tablet."

"What do you have so far?" He placed the poker stick back in its stand and sat beside her.

She ignored his powerful presence and read what she'd written. "Did I forget anything?"

He leaned closer. "Other than Leonard's name on the victim list, I don't think so."

A strand of hair slipped from her ponytail.

He pushed it behind her ear, letting his fingers linger. "You scared me today."

She gazed into his eyes and tried to read his thoughts.

I fell out of love.

His words flashed back into her mind and she popped up, walking to the window. The snowstorm had lessened, but a fresh blanket covered the already record-breaking amount of snow for this time of year.

She suppressed the urge to groan. Why couldn't she believe him? What was the emotion she continually saw in his eyes? *Friends don't look at each other like that.* Or was she just *hoping* that's what she noted. *Get a grip. Be the better person and apologize.* He only wanted to be friends. Did she really want to risk more heartbreak? No. She'd vowed to remain single and concentrate on her career. And now, Grace.

She steeled her jaw. For this case, she'd maintain distance and a working relationship for the team's sake and the innocent lives in Stittsrock Falls. She inhaled and turned back to face him. "I wanted to apologize for bringing up our broken engagement and storming out. I put you and Ziva at risk. Very unprofessional of me. It won't happen again. Can we move on?"

He looked away. "Of course. I'm sorry too." His whispered words betrayed the emotion in his voice.

She walked to the Christmas tree and fingered a reindeer ornament Grace had made at school. Memories of happier Christmases from her childhood flooded her mind. If only the season brought that same joy now. "What's the game plan for tomorrow?" When she turned back to him, she caught him staring with a distorted expression.

He shifted in his seat. "Trying to stay one step ahead of JB. I'm still curious if it was him who chased us off the road and shot at us."

"Who else would it have been? Do you have enemies you want to tell me about?" She returned to her seat and sipped her hot chocolate.

"Many, I'm afraid." He chuckled. "None come to mind at the moment. I don't have any other active cases right now." He turned back to her. "Can I ask you a question?"

What now? "After today, I'm not sure." She paused. "What do you want to know?"

"Is there something about Christmas that bothers you?"

She stilled in her seat. "Why do you ask?"

"A gut instinct. You hesitate around Christmas trees, and I remember during one season we were together, you avoided talking about Christmas."

She had never told him her secret because of her shame for walking away from God and getting pregnant. It had been years since then, but she was still embarrassed and felt distanced from God for what she'd done. For some reason, she couldn't put it behind her and move forward.

When will you trust God completely and know He works all things out?

"I just hate how society has removed Christ from Christmas and everything is about who has the biggest tree, most gifts, and best decorations." She realized it wasn't the entire truth, but her answer revealed her true feelings. "When will we get back to the basics? Back to Christ?"

You should talk.

"That's true. It seems to come earlier and earlier every year."

She yawned. "I'm heading to bed."

Zac got up and put on his jacket. "I'm going to do one sweep of the property just to be sure. Night." He turned to his partner. "Ziva, come."

The pair left the cabin, leaving Olive to wallow in her thoughts of past love and loss.

Something woke Olive with a start. She stilled, listening intently to determine what noise had stirred her from dreams of a happier life with Zac and Grace on Christmas Day. But only the wind howled outside her window. She turned her head to check on Grace on the small bed beside her. She slept soundly.

Olive registered a heaviness in her head and she reached up to touch where the airbag had hit the hardest. Was the pain from their accident? She had felt fine before bed. What had changed? Her foggy mind wouldn't allow her to comprehend more. She turned to lie on her side.

A shadow skulked across the room moments before the figure thrust a pillow over her face. She cried out and kicked with all the strength she could muster, but her body wouldn't cooperate. *Lord, help!* Once again, she kicked and rolled at the same time. It was enough to take her attacker off guard. She fell from the bed, bracing herself for a fight. She placed her hands on the footboard, rising up.

"Someone! Help!" she yelled.

Her attacker charged at her, but she found courage and dove out of his path. He thudded into the wall, knocking a picture down. It crashed, the sound resonating throughout the room.

Why wasn't anyone coming to her rescue? She looked back at Grace, who still slept soundly. "Zac! Ziva!" Confusion assaulted her, and she quickly peered around for some type of weapon to defend herself.

The suspect regained his footing and was about to charge at her when she spied a flashlight on a nearby table. She picked it up and threw it hard in his direction, hitting him in the head.

He toppled backward, slamming into a stand-up mirror. It shattered with the impact and sent slivers everywhere.

He swore and clutched his leg before staggering from the room. Seconds later, the back door opened and closed.

She had fought him off and won. For now. She ran to Grace and checked her breathing. Steady. She was sound asleep.

Olive snatched her cell phone from the nightstand and dialed 9-1-1. Something told her the others in the house required medical service. No way would Zac or Ziva not come to her rescue if they were able. *Lord, help them to be okay.*

"Nine-one-one. Do you need police, fire or ambulance?" the female operator asked.

"Police and ambulance," Olive said, dashing through the cabin. She pounded on Zac's door. "Zac!"

"Ma'am, try and stay calm. What's going on?"

Olive opened Zac's door and entered. Both he and Ziva lay motionless on the bed. "There's been an attack at the cabin on the outskirts of town." She gave the address and sprinted to Zac's bed, checking his neck for a pulse. Steady. Same as Grace.

She reached over and felt the dog's heartbeat. Strong.

Olive hazarded a guess the others in the cabin would have the same symptoms.

Except for a groggy head, she was the only conscious one. "I think someone drugged the others. Hurry, get the police and paramedics here. I fought off the attacker."

"All available units are en route. Stay calm."

Easy for you to say.

Olive knew better than to click off the call, so she threw the live phone onto the bed. She shook Zac. "Wake up, Zac!"

A door slammed, jolting Olive back into fight mode.

Had the attacker returned to finish the job?

She spied a bottle of water on his nightstand. She opened it and poured water on his face.

"Zac! Come back to me." Her heart stammered as she waited for a response. She couldn't bear the thought of losing him—a second time.

ELEVEN

A voice registered in the back of Zac's mind moments after water hit his face. Where was he? Was he dreaming? Why did his head feel so heavy?

"Zac! Wake up!"

He fluttered his eyes open.

A hazy, frantic Olly appeared in front of his face.

"Oh, thank God, you're awake," she said. "Someone is in the cabin. Where's your Glock?"

"Nightstand drawer." Zac rubbed his head and pushed himself up. "What's going on?"

"We were all drugged. Probably just enough to put you all into a deep sleep. Ziva too." She nodded at the sleeping dog.

Zac reached over and gently shook his partner. "Ziva, wake up." Nothing.

"The attacker tried to smother me, but we fought and he smashed into the mirror, breaking it. He ran out." She opened the drawer and withdrew his Glock. "A door just slammed. He might be back. I'm going to check it out." She gestured to the phone on his bed. "Nine-one-one operator is still on the call." She slowly opened the door, raising his gun.

"Olly, wait!" Zac shook his head, hoping to dislodge the fogginess in his brain. *Come on, Turner, wake up!* He placed his feet on the floor and tried to stand, but fell back on the bed. His leadlike legs wouldn't work.

I'm useless and Olly is in trouble.

Sirens sounded in the distance.

Seconds later, Olly returned with Griff and Skye by her side. "It was Griff's door, but the backyard light shows footprints in the snow leading into the woods."

"I woke from a deep sleep and heard Olive yelling. She explained what happened." Griff zippered his coat. "He might be still out there."

"I'm going with you," Skye said faintly.

"Wait, neither of you is in any condition to chase a suspect." Olly waved his Glock. "I'm more alert. I can go."

"No!" Zac willed his legs to work and stood. "Let us." He hesitated. "Wait, what about Grace?"

"I just checked on her again," Olly said. "Her pulse is still strong and her steady breathing tells me she's in a deep sleep, but I can't wake her up.

I'll get the paramedics to check on her when they arrive."

Pounding sounded at the front door.

"That's probably them now." Zac took his gun from Olly and shuffled from the room, the group following.

Zac raised his weapon. "Who is it?"

"Preston, Constable Turner."

Zac yanked open the door. "Why are you here?"

"The cabin is close to our station. We heard the 9-1-1 call over the radio and came to provide our assistance." Preston gestured to his partner. "This is Constable Neill. Ambulance is right behind us. You okay? You look a bit out of it."

Zac rubbed his temple. "Someone drugged us. My head is slowly clearing. Check the perimeter. The assailant fled about—" He turned to Olly. "How long ago?"

"Fifteen minutes," Olly replied. "He's probably long gone. Although he was wounded in our fight, so that may have slowed him down. Tracks are leading into the woods behind the cabin."

Preston unhooked his flashlight from his duty belt. "We're on it." The duo hurried from the cabin, their flashlight beams bouncing on the snow.

Seconds later, an ambulance pulled into the driveway. Brett jumped out, grabbed his bag, and ran toward them. "Zac! You okay?"

His female partner followed.

Zac stepped aside and let them enter. "Feeling groggy. We believe someone drugged us."

"Take a seat on the couch," Brett said. "This is Lesley."

She nodded and moved toward Olly. "Are you hurt?" She led her to the chair beside the fireplace and checked Olly's vitals.

Olly flailed her arms in the air. "I'm fine. Please examine Grace." She turned to Lesley. "Come with me."

"Wait, why are you so alert, Olly? What could the suspect have drugged us with?" Zac glanced toward the kitchen table in the open-concept cabin.

A discarded pizza box lay open.

Zac headed over to the table and pointed. "It must have been the pizza."

Olly's eyes widened. "That explains it. I only had a couple of bites."

"But who fed Ziva?" Zac asked, digging his fingers into his palms. Someone had gotten to his dog, and Zac wasn't happy about it.

Griff held his hands up. "Not me. I know the rules."

"I also know better than to feed Ziva," Skye said.

"Not me either," Olly said, nudging Lesley toward her room. "Please, look at Grace."

"What's going on? What's all the noise about?" Lauren shuffled into the room, rubbing her eyes.

"You okay?" Zac asked. "Looks like we were drugged and someone tried to kill Olive."

"What?" She plunked into a chair. "Is that why my head is spinning?"

Zac turned to Brett. "I'm feeling better. Attend to Lauren." A theory entered his mind, and he pivoted to address the blond analyst. "Did you feed Ziva?"

She hung her head. "I'm sorry. I did. She looked so hungry, but it was only a few bites."

Zac clenched his arms but held them by his side. "Lauren, you can't do that."

Brett knelt beside her and turned his penlight on, shining it in her eyes. "Follow the light."

She obeyed.

Griff crossed his arms. "But, Zac, how would the suspect know Lauren would feed Ziva? I think we're missing something. He would have had to guarantee the dog be incapacitated somehow."

"True." Zac checked his watch. "I need to contact our on-call vet. I don't care that it's three thirty in the morning. They have to examine Ziva."

"Do it, buddy," Griff said. "Ziva is one of us."

Zac made the call, and the vet assured him he'd be there within twenty minutes. After checking again on his sleeping dog, Zac returned to the kitchen. No way he'd be able to sleep now.

A knock sounded, and the front door opened. Preston and Constable Neill entered.

"He's gone," Preston said. "But we've called in Forensics as we found tracks in the snow."

Zac shivered from the sudden burst of cold air. "Good. Olive said he was hurt."

"Forensics should be here any minute," Constable Neill shut the door. "You all okay? I see the ambulance is still here."

"Yes, the drugs are wearing off." Griff massaged his forehead. "Hopefully, the headache subsides soon."

Zac sighed. He needed a coffee to help alleviate the pain, but knew he couldn't contaminate the scene. "Brett, can you take our blood?"

"If you all consent, I can put in an online request for testing with the emergency doctor. Once he approves, I can draw your blood. Based on your symptoms and the fact you're coming around, I'm guessing someone injected a sleeping drug into your food or drink. Let's check, to be sure." Brett scanned the room. "Do you all agree?"

They nodded.

"Okay, we'll get the request submitted." Brett secured their written consents and walked out the door to the ambulance.

A car door slammed.

Everyone's hands flew to their weapons.

Constable Neill peeked out the window. "It's okay. Forensics is here." He turned to Preston. "Let's show them what we found."

The duo left the cabin.

Olly and Lesley walked back into the living room and kitchen area.

Zac squeezed Olly's hand. "Is Grace okay?"

"She woke up for a few minutes and we moved her to Lauren's room so Forensics wouldn't disturb her. Grace was groggy but coherent. Lesley said her vitals were strong. I'm concerned about what drug they used."

"Me too. That's why I asked Brett if they could take our blood. He suspects it's some type of sleeping drug." Zac turned to Lesley. "He's submitting the request now."

"But wouldn't it be better if you all went to the hospital?" Lesley asked.

"I can't risk it. Someone is targeting our team." Zac's cell phone buzzed, and he read the screen. "The vet's here."

Zac thrust open the front door. He waited for the vet to leave his vehicle before waving him forward. "Peter, in here."

The balding man removed his bag from the front seat and sprinted into the cabin. "Where is my girl?"

"This way." Zac led him into his room.

Ziva lay on the bed, still in the same position.

"Doc, she hasn't moved." That fact alone elevated Zac's blood pressure. Concern over his dog's well-being mounted. How long before the drug wore off? Would it have lasting effects and hamper her ability to do her job effectively?

Zac grimaced as more questions arose and filled his mind with dread.

Was Ziva the actual target? Had JB wanted to wipe out the team member who could sniff out his gift bombs?

Olive paced through the house as Peter examined Ziva. She'd determined by Zac's contorted expression that he was worried about his partner. She had stood at the entrance as he'd asked the vet questions, including his suspicions on Ziva being the intended target of tonight's attack.

Could that be true? If so, why try to smother her? Perhaps they had both been the targets. Either way, Olive clenched her fists as her bulldog temperament bubbled to the surface. Sure, she had a fear of dogs, but Ziva was quickly becoming a friend, and Olive Wells protected her friends.

With her entire being.

Brett and Lesley had taken samples of their blood to be tested. The chief had told Zac he'd request they be expedited. It was vital to their investigation.

She paced the cabin, her best thinking activity. She wanted to figure out how the assailant had found them and drugged them under their noses. Right now, Zac was preoccupied and she totally understood. Ziva needed him. Grace had stirred again and Olive had given her water. She was back in bed, but awake and reading. Olive would not send her to school today. Plus, they had to move since the suspect had somehow found their cabin.

Chief Bennett had brought in extra security until they determined where to hide out. Was this all the Jingle Bell Bomber's doing? It was the only answer. She prayed the team could stay off JB's radar for a few days. They required rest and recuperation from the past twenty-four hours. If they didn't, they'd be in no shape to fight him off. She scoffed at the idea that JB would stop targeting victims while they rested.

She looked at the table. The forensics team had taken the pizza box, partially drunk pop bottles, and dirty plates to test. They'd also made footprint impressions and examined Olive's room where the suspect had attacked her earlier.

Lauren shuffled into the living room, nursing a cup of coffee. She plunked herself in the rocker by the fireplace. "Are we safe here, Olive? I don't want to die. Shouldn't we be leaving?"

The tremor in Lauren's voice confirmed the

woman's angst. Not that Olive blamed her. Their safety—especially Grace's—concerned her, but it wasn't easy to find a place to accommodate them all in this smaller town.

"Chief Bennett has more officers keeping close watch of the perimeter. No one will get by them." Well, at least she prayed that to be the case. Somehow, JB had infiltrated the premises with no one's knowledge.

"I still can't believe Fraser is gone." Tears tumbled down the analyst's cheeks.

Olive walked over to her coworker. It was true she and Lauren rarely got along, but Fraser's loss had hit Lauren hard. She required compassion. Olive squatted beside her and squeezed her hand. "I know. Were you and Fraser close?"

"I think he had a secret crush on me, but he wasn't my type." She bit her lip. "I want to go home."

Me too. "Lauren, we're safer together. Plus, I need your help with JB's ever-changing profile."

Lauren wiped her tears away, tilting her head. "You do? I thought you hated me."

"Hardly. I value your input. Yes, we've butted heads in the past, Lauren, but can we put that behind us and move on? Our profession is not a competition."

She nodded. "I'd like that. I'm sorry for how I've treated you." She paused, as if gathering her words carefully. "I just got jealous of all the attention you were getting, especially after you helped with your sister's case. I could really use a friend right now."

Olive squeezed Lauren's hand tighter. "You have one."

"Thank you."

Olive returned to her seat. "I'm wondering what drug they gave to Ziva."

"I feel terrible about giving her pizza. She only ate a couple of bites, though."

"It wasn't the pizza, Lauren." Zac returned to the living room, followed by the vet. Zac held up a bag. "We found this lodged behind her ear. JB probably shot her while we were outside."

Olive cringed at the sight of a tiny dart. "Oh, no. I'm so sorry." She addressed the vet. "Any ideas on the drug?"

"Not at the moment. Zac's team will analyze it and the blood I took from Ziva."

Olive stood and grasped Zac's arm. "Please tell me she's going to be okay."

"Peter checked her over and feels JB only gave her enough to put her into a deep sleep."

"That's right," the on-call vet said. "We'll know more, of course, when we figure out the drug type, but she's in good condition and just needs to sleep it off."

Thank You, God.

The vet zippered up his coat. "Call me if anything changes."

"I will," Zac said.

Peter left.

Lauren jumped up and flung herself into Zac's arms. "I'm so happy it wasn't the pizza."

Olive's chest tightened as irritation prickled her body. *Stop, he only wants to be friends. There will never be more.*

Zac cleared his throat and backed away. "But please refrain from feeding her. She has a specific diet."

She saluted him. "I promise."

Zac's phone buzzed and he swiped the screen. "Chief Bennett got the recording of the 9-1-1 call sending Leonard to that abandoned home. He's sending it to your email, Olly. I'm going to get Skye and Griff. Maybe between all of us, we might recognize the voice." He dashed out of the room.

A few moments later, the three entered as Olive's tablet dinged.

"Here we go." She opened the email, increased her sound level, and hit Play.

"Nine-one-one. Do you require police, fire, or ambulance services?"

"Help! My wife just fell down the stairs. She's not moving." The caller recited the address.

"Sir, I'm sending an ambulance. Can you tell me if she's breathing?"

"Hurry!"

The person clicked off.

"Great, he used a voice-changer app. That's not helpful." Skye slouched in her chair.

Why did they think JB would allow his real voice to be heard? Olive chewed on her hair and quickly dropped her hand. "Wait, this tells me something. If none of us knows JB's identity, why would he distort his voice?"

"Because at least one of us does." Zac's cell phone rang, and he checked the screen. "Hi, Chief. I'm putting you on speaker."

"Listen, the white pickup has been seen close to the cabin. We're moving you to a bungalow in a gated community. Be there in ten minutes to escort you. Stay alert." He clicked off.

Zac stuffed his phone into his pocket. "Time to move. Now."

Olive bolted from her chair. She gazed at the Christmas tree in the living room as sadness enveloped her. Grace wouldn't be happy to leave, but for now, their seasonal festivities would have to wait.

Their safety came before Christmas.

TWELVE

Two days had passed since the team had relocated to the bungalow across town. Olive sipped her coffee while staring out the back window. Thankfully, JB had also been quiet, with no further bombings. Perhaps he was also recovering from their fight and his slam into the mirror. It seemed like the calm before the storm.

The anxiousness running through Olive's body told her it was only a matter of time before he struck again. The team, including Ziva, had all recovered from the attack at the cabin. They'd discovered their drinks, not the pizza, had been laced with enough amounts of a popular sleeping drug to induce intense grogginess. Ziva's dart had also contained the same drug.

After checking with the pizza delivery company, they'd learned that they had no record of the group's order for the cabin's address. Olive guessed that somehow JB had intercepted it before the pizza restaurant could fulfill it, proving to her his skill levels included computer hacking. They had added it to the profile.

Forensics had also confirmed that the water in the library's dispenser bottle had contained high amounts of arsenic. No wonder it had induced Fraser's cardiac arrest. Also, the suspect had somehow given Leonard and his paramedic partner arsenic. They'd both been dead before the explosion even hit.

Skye and Grace had left for school earlier, leaving Olive sitting in a stilled, panicked state. Should she have kept her home? However, today was the last day before her Christmas break, and Grace didn't want to miss the Secret Santa gift exchange. She had cried when Olive had told her they had to leave the cabin, but Brynn, the brilliant and efficient station's admin, had decorated this new location. When Grace saw the clever candy cane theme, she'd squealed in delight. Olive's mind whirled with her list of Grace's presents still left to buy, silently kicking herself for not getting on it sooner.

Ziva nudged her leg, announcing her presence.

Olive rubbed the K-9's ears. "Hey, beautiful. So glad to see you up and feeling better."

Ziva barked.

"What's the commotion in here?" Zac asked, shuffling into the dining room.

"Just girl talk." Olive giggled.

Zac set a folder on the table along with his coffee cup. "Well, I can't interrupt that. Listen, the chief just sent over the foot imprint results. Our suspect has a size eleven boot, and a limp."

"Well, he may have gotten that from his crash into the mirror."

"Agreed."

Olive swiped her tablet, bringing it to life. "I'm going to update the profile and send it to all the law enforcement agencies in the area. It will help them be on the lookout."

Zac sat beside Olive and rubbed Ziva's back. "I'm really hoping we don't need to run again. It's too hard on Grace. How's she doing?"

"She was fine once she saw Brynn's new Christmas theme." Olive's cell phone rang. "It's Sergeant Alexander. I have to take this."

"I'll give you some privacy. Ziva, come." The pair left the room.

Olive hit Answer. "Sergeant. How are you?"

"Wife has me shopping for her parents. My favorite thing to do." He chuckled. "I wanted to check in with you. I know Fraser's death has been hard. How are you and Lauren doing?"

"Surviving. Lauren took it hard, but it's brought us closer together. That's one good thing." Olive ran her finger along her coffee cup.

"I have more information for you and the team. We've determined how JB got into our cameras."

Olive braced herself for bad news. "How?"

"Definitely a virus, but, Olive, they somehow attached it to an email you sent the team."

She jerked her hand, knocking her coffee cup over. "What? How?" Suddenly, her coffee hardened in her stomach.

"I'm thinking JB somehow got into your laptop and planted it, so when you emailed the team, you unleashed it."

Olive snatched up a napkin and wiped the coffee. "Well, we've determined he hacked into the pizza company records, so I'm not surprised he could do that too. He's smart. The car accident destroyed my laptop. Zac's chief set me up with another tablet." Olive rubbed the back of her neck. Tension turned her muscles rock-solid.

"Good. I just wanted to check up on you and Lauren and let you know about the virus. Thanks for sending me your update. Keep them coming."

"Of course."

"Stay safe." He hung up.

Olive tossed her phone on the table. They needed to stop this maniac. She stared at the victim's pictures on their board, shifting her concentration back to the mysterious combination of careers. *Show me what their link is, Lord. Before JB strikes again.* She reviewed each face and occupation carefully. After brainstorming last night and even putting their names in the police's database, the team found no leads. There had to be one. JB wouldn't pick them randomly. Would he?

She buried her head in her hands as frustration tightened her chest. *You have to solve this.* Doubts filled her mind as she racked her brain for answers. Any answers.

Harried footsteps raised her nerves and she sat upright.

Zac ran into the room, holding up his phone. "Chief Bennett just called. The team cracked through the pickup's shell corporation and it's registered to the school board. More specifically to Principal Bell."

"What?" Olive's cell phone buzzed, startling her. She fished it out and peered at the screen.

A picture of Grace playing in the snow at recess popped up with a text.

Will someone get hurt playing Secret Santa? Don't trust the gifts under the tree. Only Zac and Ziva may play this round of the game.

"No!" She grabbed Zac's arm. "We must get to the school. Now!"

Olive wouldn't lose the best thing that had happened to her in months.

The little girl she now called a daughter needed her help.

* * *

Zac's cruiser skidded as he steered into Grace's school parking lot. They had called in the bomb unit and alerted Constable Lynch to the danger. The freezing temperatures had prompted Lynch to evacuate the kids and take refuge in the aquatic center across the street from the school. Zac sent a fellow officer to detain the principal under a false premise. He didn't want her frightened. Just in case she was the Jingle Bell Bomber or knew his identity.

He snuck a peek at Olly.

She chewed on a strand of hair but dropped it when she caught his look. "Bad habit, I know."

"I think it's adorable." Did he just say that out loud?

She turned back and gazed out the window. "What's the game plan?"

She ignored his comment, but he didn't blame her. He'd made it clear they'd only be friends. Zac wished it wasn't so, but his father severed any hope of a relationship.

"You join Skye at the center. Ziva and I will search the school." He hated to not go with her, but his fellow well-trained constable would protect Olly with her life. "You still have my backup Glock?"

She patted her winter coat pocket. "I do. Let's go." She reached for the door but hesitated. "Please be careful."

"I will. You too." Zac released his K-9 from the rear of his vehicle. He grabbed his equipment and put on his bomb suit to protect himself.

Zac waited until Olly safely entered the aquatic center before addressing his dog. "Ziva, come."

They entered the school cautiously. Silence greeted them. Thankfully, everyone had been evacuated and the bomb unit would arrive soon. It was up to his partner to find the bomb.

Zac squatted in front of her, praying she was up to the task. The drug was gone from her system and her strength returned, but had it affected her scent cone? *Trust.* She had passed his earlier test, so Zac needed to put his faith in his partner. He rubbed her ears. "Let's do this, girl." He stood. "Ziva, seek."

The dog raced down the corridor and entered the first classroom. She reappeared a minute later, showing she had not detected any explosives. She continued to the next room, repeating the same process.

Zac stayed at the door of a third room, studying his partner search. The desk nameplate sitting by the computer read "Principal Bell." Had she been targeted or was she somehow connected to this sick, deadly game?

Sirens outside told Zac the bomb unit had arrived. Not that he wasn't capable of disarming a device, but he could use the additional help.

Ziva sniffed the desk, the credenza, then around the office perimeter. She came out the door and immediately went back inside to the credenza.

She sat.

Her process of alerting.

The bomb was inside the credenza.

Zac brought out Ziva's ball. "Come."

She obeyed. "Good girl. Stay." He dropped the ball into her mouth before moving farther into the room, inching toward the credenza. He slowly opened the drawer and peered inside.

A Christmas gift with a bow sat on top of a stack of papers. A tag attached to the bow held a message.

This one will go boom. JB

Zac carefully examined the gift with his tools and determined the absence of trip wires. He gently lifted the lid, revealing a pipe bomb with a digital clock.

The timer read 5:00.

Seconds later, it changed to 4:59 and began descending.

Zac's head throbbed and he unclipped his radio, pressing the button. "Constable Turner here. Ziva alerted. Bomb is in the principal's office. Top credenza drawer. Timer is counting down—4:58 minutes." He set his watch to match the bomb's detonation clock.

"Copy that, Turner," Constable Pike said. "Stand down. We'll move in."

The hairs on the back of Zac's neck prickled. Great. Pike grated on everyone's nerves, including Zac's. The man always had to defuse the bomb and save the day himself.

However, his seniority trumped Zac's.

"Ziva, come." Zac exited the room and scurried down the corridor.

A noise stopped him in his tracks beside the stairwell.

Whistling sounded from below.

Ziva barked.

She sensed the danger too.

Same tune the school janitor, Brad, had whistled before. The janitor was still in the building.

Zac looked at his watch. Minutes to detonation: 3:50.

The unit would be busy with the bomb.

It was up to Zac and Ziva to get Brad out, but something niggled at him. Was the janitor involved?

Zac set the question aside and darted down the steps.

Olive checked her phone for an update from Zac while glancing out the front window. It had been almost ten minutes since they'd separated, each with a specific task, but yet it felt like an eternity. *Lord, keep him and Ziva safe.* Having him return to her life—even for a short time-frame—had brought her feelings plunging back. She'd be devastated if something happened to either of them. The bomb unit entered the school in full gear. She drew in a sharp breath. Had Ziva found something? She kept her eye on the door, but Zac didn't come out. Was he trying to defuse the bomb?

Once again, she checked her phone and willed it to ring. Text. Anything from Zac. But nothing came.

She needed a distraction.

Grace and her fellow students huddled in the corner, drawing Christmas pictures. Thankfully, the center had a playroom and ample supplies to keep the children occupied while they waited for their parents to pick them up. Principal Bell was contacting them personally. All employees were taking refuge in the center.

The school would likely be officially closed for the Christmas break. Skye hovered close by, protecting the children.

Olive approached the group and sat on the floor next to Grace. "Hey, Ladybug. Let me see your picture?"

Grace raised her drawing.

She'd drawn a scene of a Christmas tree with Ziva lying under it and a little girl petting the dog. A man and woman held hands in the background.

Olive gulped. It was a family picture.

Of them.

This wasn't the distraction Olive wanted.

"Isn't it pretty?" Grace asked.

"Beautiful. Who is it?"

"Silly, it's us, Ziva, and Mr. Zac. I like him." She went back to finishing the drawing.

Olive smothered the cry, wanting to escape. *I do too, Ladybug. Too much.* If only—

Skye's cell phone rang, interrupting Olive's thoughts. Skye had positioned herself at the door, guarding the children from a distance. After taking the call, her expression changed to distress, and she pivoted.

Olive guessed it was to hide her face from what the caller had said and Olive wanted—no, needed—to know. She pushed herself up and moved over to where the constable stood.

Skye turned, but held up her index finger. "How many minutes?" Her eyes widened.

That doesn't sound good.

"Copy that. Keep me updated." Skye punched off.

"What's going on?"

Her friend averted her gaze.

Olive squeezed her arm. "Tell me. You know I'm on the team."

"That was Constable Pike. He's onsite trying to defuse the bomb, but there are only two minutes left on the timer."

Olive's legs buckled and she clung to the wall to steady herself. "Where are Zac and Ziva?"

"Apparently on their way out, Zac heard someone whistling, so he's trying to locate that person. He thinks it's Brad the janitor."

No! She fished her cell phone from her jacket pocket. "I'm calling him."

"Olive, don't interrupt him. He knows what he's doing. Ziva too."

Olive pointed to the man sitting in the room's corner. "That's Brad! It's a trap! Zac has to get out." Her voice elevated, catching the children's attention. *Stupid, Olive.* She had only been thinking about the safety of Zac and his dog. "Call them." This was no coincidence. The Jingle Bell Bomber had orchestrated the entire ruse to keep Zac in the building. She doubted the countdown was accurate. So far, JB had been unpredictable and she wouldn't put it past him to trick them all to eliminate the entire team because they were impeding his game.

Skye hit her radio button. "Zac, Pike, get out. It's a trap. Have it on good authority the timer is wrong."

"Who's authority?" Pike's voice boomed.

"Trust me, Pike. She's good at profiling people."

Pike mumbled. "You mean Wells, don't you? We still have two minutes."

His tone told Olive the man didn't like profilers.

"We don't have time for this, Skye." She snatched the radio from her friend. "Listen to me, I've been studying JB and I'm beginning to see how he thinks. He's a trickster and wants the team gone so he can eliminate everyone from his naughty list. He's rigged the countdown to give you the wrong time, or he's watching from somewhere. Trust me, he's going to blow the building. Get out of there. Now!"

She prayed Zac listened in on the conversation. But why hadn't he responded? She pressed the button again. "Zac, I hope you can hear me. Get out. You need—"

An explosion shook the building.

Lord, no!

She turned to leave, but Skye pulled her back. "Stay here. JB is out there."

Olive retrieved the Glock from her pocket. "I have a weapon."

"Good. Keep a close watch on the kids." Skye took her radio from Olive. "I'm calling for backup."

Olive's pulse zinged, sending her heart into overdrive. She willed it to slow down because right now the children in the room depended on her, especially Grace.

THIRTEEN

Zac's ears rang as he struggled to register exactly where he and Ziva were located inside the building. The whistling had led them into the basement just as Olly's desperate plea had told him to get out. He'd commanded Ziva to heel seconds before the explosion hit, and had thrown himself on top of his K-9 partner. The blast debris now blocked their exit, burying them in the lower level. Thankfully, he and Ziva had been far enough away from the blast center to survive, even though they were trapped.

"Ziva, you okay, girl?" Zac pushed debris aside and eased himself up. The ringing in his ears silenced, but his head wouldn't stop the excessive pounding. He removed his helmet and brushed his forehead, fingering a goose egg forming.

Zac drew in a long breath and exhaled to calm himself and stop the storm hammering in his head. Questions plagued him. Did Pike's team get out in time? Had JB kept Zac in the building as a ruse to take him and Ziva out? Zac remembered the bomber's earlier comment about dogs. Why would his opinion change? Were Zac and Ziva a threat to him fulfilling his plan?

Zac set aside the questions and shone his flashlight on his partner's body, searching for flesh wounds while praying he wouldn't find any. He ran his hands down her legs.

Ziva whimpered.

Oh no! Her yelp told him her leg hurt. Zac needed to get Ziva to the vet, but that required them to vacate their prison. He pressed his radio button. "Anyone hear me? We're trapped in the basement."

The airways crackled, but no reply followed.

He tried again. "Pike? Griff? Lynch?"

The explosion had blocked his communication from the basement. He studied the stairs and down the corridor. The blast had also taken out the power, leaving him in darkness. His chest tightened as a tingling sensation fluttered through his legs into his feet, weakening his stance. The urgency to flee consumed him, but his body froze. He sank to the floor as his heart rate increased. What was happening to him? Is this what it felt like to have a panic attack? He'd never had such overwhelming anxiety erupt for tight spaces.

Lord, help me.

Ziva whined and struggled to move closer, as if sensing Zac's distress. She nudged her nose into Zac's face.

His dog knew he needed her. Even with her injuries, Ziva's presence helped to lessen his panicked state. His heart rate decreased as strength returned to his limbs. God used Ziva to answer his desperate appeal.

Zac took his K-9's face in his hands, kissing her forehead. "You knew, didn't you? You're a good girl." He rubbed her back. "Okay, it looks like it's up to us to get out." Once again, he stood.

Ziva barked, eased herself up and limped slowly down the corridor.

She'd caught a scent of some kind. Her canine instincts were on alert.

Zac unhooked a flashlight from his duty belt and followed his partner down the darkened hall. He peered into the janitor's office. Empty. A tape recorder perched on his desk's corner intrigued him. He pressed Play. Whistling sounded and Zac stiffened. It had been a trap to bring them to the basement. But why?

Zac stuck it in his pocket and kept moving, passing a supply closet, electrical room and equipment area. Ziva hadn't stopped at any of those, so Zac guessed they weren't the object of her quest. He inched farther into the darkness of the older school as questions filled his mind about why JB would blow up a building harboring innocent children—or had his target been a specific teacher?

His partner barked in the distance.

Zac sidestepped debris and hurried toward Ziva.

Seconds later, he found her sitting in front of a partly demolished wall. Why alert to this spot?

"What is it, girl?"

Zac shone his light around the broken drywall and stopped at a hole. He peered closer as a slight breeze blew in his face, showing an opening behind the wall. Zac tugged at the drywall and a chunk fell away, revealing a boarded-up door. Someone had sealed off a room in this aged school. Why?

He turned to Ziva. "What did you find, girl?"

She whimpered and sank to the floor.

Zac had to get her out; perhaps an exit hid behind the door. Why else would she alert to it? He doubted JB would have planted a bomb and sealed it in. Wasn't his MO. First, Zac required a tool to finish tearing it down. He remembered the janitor's office and pivoted to retrace his steps.

A rumble sent a tremor throughout the lower level, showering more drywall and chunks of cement in his path. Zac dropped to the floor. Dust rained down on him, stealing what already poisoned air was left in the compromised area. He held his breath as he waited for the building to settle. Moments later, it stilled. Zac continued forward as an elevated determination took over. They must escape the basement before the entire building collapsed.

Zac entered the janitor's room. He shone his light around until he found a closet and opened it. A sledgehammer leaned against the corner. He grabbed it and raced back to Ziva's location.

Zac lifted the sledgehammer and thrust it into the wall, over and over, until he broke through, creating an opening big enough to crawl into. He shone his flashlight into the hole.

A small, hidden, dungeon-like room appeared, containing a rusted cot, broken toilet and sink, two old-fashioned school desks, and a bookshelf. A musty odor assaulted his nose, and he clamped his hand over his mouth. His earlier question resurfaced. Why hide this room? He continued to move the light around until he noticed a cement staircase in the far corner. Zac gasped. Was this a way out of their enclosed underground prison?

Another vibration rumbled throughout the basement, urging him forward. He glanced at Ziva. Her breathing was now labored. Zac squatted in front of her. "Ziva, I've got you." He scooped his partner up and carried her over his shoulder, stumbling toward the staircase. Using his free hand, he shone his flashlight upward. A partially broken door with a rusted, shattered, chain lock stood at the top of the chipped cement steps, but the boarded exit concealed the entire entrance. He set Ziva down, ran back and snatched the sledgehammer before returning to their possible escape route.

Would his deteriorating energy and the heavy bomb suit allow him to even lift the tool to break through the door? *Give me strength, Lord.* He lugged the hammer up the stairs, keeping to the right, close to the wall, for fear of the steps collapsing. After reaching the top, he released the broken chain and opened the door, exposing a second one. He turned the handle, but it was locked from the outside.

Zac marshaled his strength and lifted the sledgehammer, ramming it into the wood repeatedly until the heavy oak splintered. He continued until the hole grew big enough for them to evacuate. He sprinted back to Ziva and gathered her before stepping through the broken exit, gulping in much-needed fresh air. In. Out. In. Out.

Zac peered upward into an enormous wall of dense cedar trees, obstructing his view of anything beyond it. Clearly, it had aided in hiding the secret entrance all these years. The question remained—what were they hiding?

Zac ignored the lingering mystery and parted

the branches, pushing his way through the wall of secrets, lugging his injured partner.

They made it to the other side and Zac stopped short.

He was behind the school's property, concealed from everyone.

He trudged through the deep snow and made his way to a back road.

Zac turned to study the building and wobbled.

How had they survived the explosion?

The school had been flattened. The basement had saved their lives. Was that why someone had lured them there? To save them and expose the secret room?

A sudden desire to find Olly overpowered him and he found strength before blundering down the road, being careful not to jostle Ziva in his arms. They made it to the aquatic center just as the door flung open and Olly appeared.

"Zac! Ziva!" she yelled, flinging her arms around both of them. "You're alive."

He buried his face in her embrace, choking back tears of emotions threatening to expel. He thought he'd never see her again after the explosion hit.

And that had scared him to death.

Olive's nerves had fluttered and accelerated at the sight of Zac holding Ziva as he had staggered down the side street. She screamed and shot out the front, throwing herself at him. She was scared the blast had killed him alongside a bomb unit member. The concept of losing Zac forever sent tremors of dread throughout her body. "I thought I lost you." She buried her head in his chest, tears running down her cheeks. She realized he only wanted to be friends, but the idea of him being killed sent her feelings pummeling back.

Zac's body tightened, and then he broke their hold. "I'm okay, but I must get Ziva out of the cold. She's hurt. Plus, I'm sure JB is watching."

Olive rubbed the dog's forehead to distract herself and hide the emotion plaguing her face. "Let's go. You can tell me what happened inside." She ran toward the door, glimpsing at the school. Firefighters struggled to get the blaze under control. The explosion had obliterated the building, but flames had ignited nearby trees. They tried to stop it from spreading through the neighborhood homes.

Zac's footfalls halted behind her.

She turned.

He stared at the leveled school building, his mouth gaping open.

She tugged on his arm. "Come on, Zac. There's nothing more you can do. The school is gone." She opened the door and nudged him through.

Zac followed her into the room allotted to their

group and set Ziva on top of a small table in the corner, rubbing her leg. "Did the bomb unit evacuate? Your cry told me to get out, but we were in the basement and got buried in rubble. Ziva hurt her leg."

"Pike wouldn't listen to me. Here, sit." Olive lugged a chair over. "I figured out it was a trap and JB would detonate the bomb before the clock ran out."

Zac wiggled out of his heavy bomb suit. "How did you know?"

"Pike said you thought the janitor was in the building. I'd just seen Brad and knew something was wrong."

Parents pushed through the doorway, racing toward their children. Skye spoke to each before they scooped up their child and left.

Moments later, Skye approached. "Zac, so glad you're okay." She gestured to the last parent leaving the room. "I assured them their children are all safe."

"What's the update? Did the unit get out in time?" Zac asked.

"Most did, but we lost one of Pike's men and it was Pike's fault." She pursed her lips. "He wouldn't listen to Olive."

Zac's face reddened. "Not surprised. He probably thought he could disarm it and save the day."

Chief Bennett bolted into the room, beelining toward them. "Zac, you guys okay? What happened?"

"Fine." Zac rubbed dust from Ziva's back. "This girl found an escape route for me, but she's hurt and must be taken to the vet ASAP." Zac explained how the whistling led them to the basement. When he'd heard Olive's pleas, he'd started back up the stairs, but the blast had prevented his getaway. He handed the chief the tape recorder and also explained how Ziva had found a secret room that had led to their escape.

Olive squeezed his shoulder. "Being in the basement saved your and Ziva's life. God protected you."

A shadow passed over his face for a split second. He had believed. What changed that?

Chief Bennett crossed his arms. "I don't understand why he'd blow up the school. What did it gain?"

"Could there be a connection to the secret room?" Skye asked. "Maybe he knew about it."

"It appeared to be a student's classroom, but someone boarded it up and dry-walled over the entrance to hide it." Zac stood and addressed Olive. "Where's Lauren?"

"Back at the safe house, going over the files." She drew in a quick breath. "Griff is with her. Is she safe?"

"I'm sure she's fine. Griff is a solid officer." Zac

turned to Skye. "Get Grace back to the house. We have to talk to Principal Bell. She knows something."

Olive's cell phone buzzed. Unknown Caller. She clutched Zac's arm. "I'm guessing this is probably him."

"I'll see if we can get a trace." Chief Bennett withdrew his phone and made a call.

"Put it on speaker, Olly." Zac turned to Skye. "Please get Grace out of here now. I don't want this call to scare her."

Skye nodded and gathered up Grace's things before they both departed.

Olive punched Answer and then hit the speaker button. "Olive Wells here."

"It's about time you answered," the distorted voice said. "You guys aren't playing my game correctly."

"What did we do wrong?" Olive tightened her grip on the phone.

"Easy. You sent in the bomb unit."

"You can't expect us not to involve them. They are trained. Why did you destroy the school?" Olive asked, heat assaulting her face. She inhaled to curb the anger from escalating further. "You could have hurt those children."

"I would never do that. I waited until they were out, but you saved them." He cleared his throat. "Constable Turner, glad you survived. I hope

Ziva isn't hurt too badly. I guess luring you into the basement kept you alive."

Zac's expression hardened. "Why, JB?"

"Things that happened in the school needed to be buried. Forever."

Olive jerked her gaze to Zac's. "What does that mean?"

"Ask Principal Bell. She knows."

Click.

A thought formed in Olive's mind.

This case just got even more complicated.

"What are you hiding? We've linked a white pickup, recently spotted at a crime scene, back to you and your school." Zac observed the principal with a heightened sense. He wanted to scrutinize each expression passing over her face.

After JB's call, Zac had quickly cleaned himself up in a nearby washroom and the chief had taken Ziva to the vet. Zac had hated to leave his partner and still struggled with the decision, but JB had targeted them, and Zac still had work to do, so they'd set up a makeshift interrogation room at the aquatic center. They'd cleared all other personnel from the area. The chief had reported the call wasn't long enough for them to determine JB's location.

Zac resisted the urge to pound the table at the frustration overpowering his exhausted body.

They needed a break in this case before they lost more innocent lives.

Olly sat next to him, leaning forward. Her fierce gaze told Zac she also dissected the woman's every move.

Principal Bell shifted in her chair. "I—I don't know what you're talking about. I don't own a pickup. White or otherwise."

"What about your janitor?" Olly asked.

"Not that I'm aware of. Brad drives a red sedan."

Had JB hacked into records and switched the pickup's registration information? Another dead end. Time to change tactics. "Why is there a room concealed and dry-walled shut in the school's basement? What was it used for?" Zac failed to keep his voice from revealing the anger surfacing. This woman knew something, and he was determined to find out what.

The principal bit her lip. "Have you spoken to Mr. Longy?"

"Why? Should we?" Olly quirked a brow at Zac.

Obviously, she also struggled to find a link between the school and the Jingle Bell Bomber. Nothing made sense.

Zac shifted in his chair, trying not to let his irritation show in his body or facial expression. "Tell us why we should, Principal Bell."

She looked around before inching forward in her chair, her wrinkled face grimacing. "Because he was the one who boarded it up." Her whispered words spoke volumes.

A secret lay hidden deep in the school's history.

What? Heat flushed Zac's body. "When was this?"

"Five years ago." The woman's eyes darted to the entranceway.

"What are you scared of?" Olly asked.

"It's not what but who." Principal Bell's voice quivered. "I didn't mean for them to pressure me to do it."

Whatever this school hid must have been the reason JB destroyed it.

You saved them.

JB's words tumbled back through Zac's mind. Who was he referring to?

Principal Bell and—

Zac sprang out of his chair and paced the room. He had to think, and he did it best when walking. He rubbed his temples, hoping to clear his foggy brain after being trapped in the school's basement. His mind envisioned the tiny boarded-up room.

Cot, school desks, bookshelves.

He sucked in a ragged breath and stopped pacing, turning to face the principal. "You detained students in the basement years ago, didn't you?"

And one of those students had been the Jingle Bell Bomber.

That's why he'd destroyed the school.

Justice.

Olive's jaw dropped as she searched Zac's face. His handsome features had blanched at the possibility of the principal holding students away from the rest of the children. Exactly what terrible deeds had warranted them to be separated from their friends? *Grace goes to this school. Lord, protect the kids.* Olive closed her fists to bury her anger for this woman and waited for her reply.

Principal Bell hissed a breath through her teeth. "The board made us do it."

Zac placed his hands on the table and leaned into the woman's personal space. "Who are 'us' and what exactly did you do?"

The woman's pasty, wrinkled face froze. Seconds later, a fat tear spilled. "Twenty-five years ago, we had a few unruly children that acted up, bullying other kids. The parents were livid and demanded we do something about it, so I took it to the board. They ordered us to use the abandoned old detention center in the basement to separate the kids."

Olive recoiled in her chair. "How did no one else know about this? The kids didn't complain?"

"We warned them not to or there would be re-percussions."

"You mean like a ruler across their knuckles?" Zac asked.

The principal nodded. "I didn't want to do it, but the board said if I didn't, I'd be fired. I was a single mother and needed the job."

"So you sacrificed the welfare of a few children to save your own hide?" Olive asked.

"Yes, it was wrong, and I deeply regret my actions." She wiped her full-blown tears from her cheeks.

"How many kids did you detain in your dungeon?" Zac asked as he typed on his cell phone.

"Too many to remember." The woman got up and walked to the window.

"Anyone else involved?" Olive struggled with how a school would allow such actions.

"Only myself and Brad."

"So, he was your accomplice all these years, but yet he boarded the room up. Why?" Zac moved closer to the woman.

"Five years ago, he found God." She shook her head. "He wouldn't come forward because he loved me. Said he wouldn't sacrifice me. So, we hid the crimes. Well, we assumed we did."

"Give us the names of every child you kept in the basement," Zac said.

"I don't remember, and we didn't keep records

back then." She waved her hand in the air, as if dismissing their crimes and exonerating herself.

As if that were possible.

But what was the connection to their case?

Olive folded her arms, tapping her fingers on her biceps. Then she halted and sat straighter. "Wait—the bomber targeted you both today, not the bomb unit. Correct?"

Principal Bell's face blanched before turning to gaze out the window.

The woman realized Olive's statement was true.

A thought slipped through Olive's mind. "You detained the child we now recognize as the Jingle Bell Bomber, didn't you? He wanted to kill you and destroy the secret room in the basement."

The principal turned, her distorted face disappeared and was replaced with a look of joy. "Basement? What are you talking about, dear? Is it time for lunch yet?" She fiddled with the ties on her sleeves.

Olive flew out of her chair. She knew the signs from her own mother.

This woman struggled with Alzheimer's.

A thought bull-rushed Olive. JB's identity was locked in the principal's broken mind. That meant *she* was the target today. "Zac, we have to protect—"

Pfft.

A bullet fractured a hole in the window, silencing Olive's words.

Principal Bell dropped to the floor.

Gunshot to the temple.

JB hadn't been able to take the woman out with a bomb, so he'd used a rifle instead.

FOURTEEN

Multiple bullets crashed through the window and shattered the glass. Zac sank to the ground, unholstering his Glock. "Olly, get down!"

Zac raised his weapon and peeked through the exposed window. A gust of wind snaked into the room, plummeting the temperature and bringing a flash freeze. JB had killed today's intended target and now wanted to make sure whatever she'd told them died with them as well.

But Zac would not let that happen. He placed his fingers on the principal's neck. No pulse. She was gone. He hit his radio button. "Shots fired. Send all available units to Stittsrock Falls aquatic center. One elderly female deceased. Sniper is at large." He clicked off and waited.

"Copy that," Dispatch said.

Zac waited for more gunfire, but none came. He turned his gaze to Olly. "You okay?"

She'd flattened herself in the corner to evade

the bullets' trajectories. "Tired of being attacked. Principal Bell?"

"I'm afraid she's gone. She was definitely today's target."

"Agreed," Olly said. "But how does she connect to the other victims? I get he wanted her sins to be exposed, but how does his game link back to the others?"

"Good question." Zac eyed Principal Bell's lifeless body. "I'm afraid any knowledge died with her."

"Plus, how much of it was accurate? You saw her reaction at the end. Zac, I know the signs. She had Alzheimer's or an early onset of it. My mother was the same way. One minute she was alert, the next she'd forgotten what we were talking about."

"How did the principal keep her job?"

"I'm guessing she was probably just diagnosed and learned how to hide it." Olly glanced at the floor, biting a strand of hair. "Just like Mom did. Plus, Dad—" Her gaze averted back to him, eyes widening. "Wait, I bet Brad helped conceal her illness, especially if he loved her. We have to find him."

"Didn't you say you saw him earlier?"

"Yes, but that was before the blast."

Sirens blared through the broken window, announcing help.

Zac eased himself up. "Shooter has to be gone. Let's update the team and find Brad."

Two hours later, after being checked out by paramedics, they were back at the bungalow. Thankfully, Ziva had only had a minor sprain. The vet had wrapped her leg and given her something for the pain, but wanted to watch her for a bit. He'd explained she would be ready to return to work in a few hours, but cautioned against strenuous running. The chief had reported the recording device was another dead end as no fingerprints were lifted and it only contained the whistling sound clip.

Zac had shared with the team everything about Principal Bell and the school's secret, including their suspicion JB had been one of the children locked in the basement classroom. They had failed to find Brad Longy at his home address and Zac had issued a BOLO—Be on the Lookout—for the man.

Zac suspected the janitor had gone into hiding after the building destruction. He'd probably guessed JB's identity and knew he was now in danger of becoming the bomber's next target.

A question plagued Zac. What was JB's motive? Surely, being detained in a basement room wasn't behind his deadly jingle bell game. There had to be more.

Time to connect the dots of their puzzling case. But, how? He tapped his pen.

"What are you thinking?" Olly asked.

She had consulted with Lauren on today's events and updated JB's profile with the new information. The team sat together now, discussing the case. Skye and Grace were busy working on a Christmas puzzle in the living room. Olly had told Zac she wanted the six-year-old to stay preoccupied for the rest of her Christmas break.

"I'm frustrated about how to connect the school's secret to JB's case. Surely, these killings aren't because he was allegedly locked in a room as a part of his discipline. I wish they'd kept better records. We have to find Brad. He might be the key."

"Does he have family here in Stittsrock Falls?" Griff asked.

"Good question. He doesn't have any type of record. Let's check social media." Zac fired up his laptop and entered Brad's name in the search engine. "Lots of choices."

Olly scooted her chair closer. "Let me see."

Her cinnamon scent wafted in the room, tickling his nose and thrusting him back to their first date when they had gone to the movies. She had worn the same fragrance.

"Zac? Where did you just go?" Olly asked.

Get with it, Turner. You know you can't go back there.

"Sorry, what did you say?" Zac edged away from the woman beside him, distancing himself from further regret. This case demanded his total focus and daydreaming about their past relationship had to end. Now.

She pointed. "I wanted you to click on this social media account. That looks like Brad the janitor."

Zac pressed the link and scrolled down the man's profile. He stopped on a post from yesterday. "Look at this. 'Big things are happening tomorrow. Stay tuned for pics.' What do you think it means?"

Lauren closed her folder and tossed it aside. "My eyes are going buggy looking at these files. Are you proposing Brad is JB?"

Olly shook her head. "He doesn't fit the age bracket of our profile."

Lauren huffed before sipping her tea. "But what about the old typewriter? Plus, what big thing would he be referring to if it wasn't the school bombing?"

Olly stood and paced around the table. "Well, today was their Secret Santa exchange at the school. Perhaps that?"

"We're all guessing now. We need facts." Zac clicked on Brad's profile details and whistled.

"Here we go. Looks like he has a sister. Beth Longy, but she lives in Alberta."

"Can you check your database? Maybe his sister has a record." Olly sat back down.

Lauren walked over and peered at Zac's screen. "You feel this little old lady is a criminal?"

Zac typed her name in the database search field. "Anything is possible, Lauren." Seconds later, a hit came up on his screen. "Well, well. Beth Longy. Age 81. Arrested thirty years ago for kidnapping a child."

"What?" Olly peered closer. "Says she denied it. That she was just helping a friend hide the child against her abusive father."

"Does it give her current address and phone number?" Griff asked. "Maybe we can call her. See if she's heard from her brother."

Zac switched to another screen and checked. "Right here." He set his cell phone on the table and dialed the number. "Let me ask the questions. Okay?"

The group nodded.

"Hello?" a weakened voice said.

"This is Stittsrock Falls Constable Zac Turner. Is this Beth Longy?"

"Yes. What do you want, Constable?"

He ignored her harsh tone. "We're looking for your brother, Brad. I realize you're in Alberta, but has Brad contacted you recently?"

She let out some derogatory names in between curse words. "Hardly. We don't keep in touch any longer. What has he done this time?"

Zac leaned forward. "Why do you ask, Miss Longy?"

"He was always a troublemaker when we were young."

Zac shifted in his seat. He required more information. "I heard he became a Christian. People change."

"Not sure I believe that. Check with his girlfriend. The principal lady."

"I'm afraid she's deceased. Do you know where he might run to hide? Old family home? Friend's house?" Zac asked.

"Mom and Dad used to own a farm outside the city, but it's abandoned. They never sold it." She gave the address. "Is that all? I'm napping and I need to go back to sleep."

Lauren chuckled before she clamped her hand over her mouth.

"Thank you for your time, Miss Longy. Have a good day." He punched off the call. "Olly, I need you where I can keep a close eye on you. Let's go check out this address Beth gave us. Lauren, stay here with Griff."

Lauren puckered her lips. "You guys have all the fun." She raised her hands. "Kidding. Stay safe. I'll check in with Sergeant Alexander to see if he has any updates."

"Awesome, thanks, Lauren." Olly lifted her coat from the coat-tree and stepped into her boots.

Zac put on his parka and opened the front door. Large wind gusts snaked inside as snowflakes blew into the foyer.

Great. Not only were they fighting a serial bomber, but now another storm.

Olive clung to the door's grab handle as Zac's cruiser skidded on the snow-covered, icy road. The drive to Brad's family farm was taking longer than expected, as the storm had hit quickly with a vengeance. It had been the second storm within four days. Normally, she wouldn't care, but her joy of partaking in winter activities had dissipated alongside her faith in God. She'd become numb and failed to move past the grief of losing Zac. Why couldn't she trust in God's strength to help her through? After all, she'd lectured many times about having faith—in all circumstances. *You're such a fraud.*

A car horn brought her back to the moment. *Focus.*

"It's so hard to see what road to take," Zac said. "Maybe this was a mistake venturing out in another storm. Although, I know how much you love snow. Perhaps we could build a snow-man with Grace later?"

Her eyes jerked to his before switching back to the window. "Maybe."

"Olly, what is it? I feel you're hiding something."

"Me, hiding something? You still won't say why you really called off our engagement." Bad move. Why did she keep bringing up the subject?

Only the snow pounding the windshield loomed, filling the car with awkward silence.

Now you've gone and done it. You need to work with this man. JB kept changing things up, so she wanted to stay close and provide her profiler's insight. She would not let him kill more innocent people. "Sorry, I shouldn't have said anything." When would her stubborn nature let things go?

"I guess we both have secrets we hold close."

She pointed. "There's the road."

Zac took a sharp right, the vehicle fishtailing.

Olive braced herself as Zac struggled to keep the cruiser steady. Thankfully, the side road was absent of other vehicles.

Zac swerved the vehicle back into the right lane. "Sorry about that." He rubbed his gloved fingers over the frost on the windshield's interior. "Getting harder to see."

"There's the farmhouse." Olive peered out her

window. "Definitely looks abandoned. No one has plowed."

"We'll park alongside the road and go on foot. I have snowshoes in the back." Zac parked and hit the hazard lights.

Olive tugged her tuque on and zipped her coat tighter to her neck before stepping outside the cruiser.

The wind bit at her face and she regretted not bringing her flannel scarf.

The house's missing shingles left gaping holes. Broken veranda posts had fallen into the door, leaving the house wide open. It appeared no one had visited this abandoned home in years, but the fractured entrance left it accessible for intruders and animals. She turned back to Zac. "I doubt he's here."

"Agreed, but we still have to check it out. I wish Ziva was here, but we must find Brad." He took out snowshoes and handed her a pair. "Put these on. It will make the walk easier." He flung his bag over his shoulder.

She obeyed, and moments later, they made their way across the snow-covered front yard. She stopped when they reached the veranda. Extensive holes on the deck prevented them from venturing further. "Now what?"

"Let's circle the premises before entering that rickety house."

They relocated to the rear of the property and stopped at the sight of a newly constructed portable shed sitting on a raised post-and-beam structure.

Tracks led from the tree line to the shed.

The house was abandoned, but the updated building revealed current activity.

What would they find inside?

"Zac, what do we do now?" she asked.

He squatted and pointed. "There are fresh tracks leading into the shed. Looks like someone was just here. I want a closer look."

He walked up the steps and fingered the lock. It fell open. "Brad might be in there and in danger." He shone his flashlight around the doorframe. "No trip wires. I'm going inside."

"Be careful, Zac!" She bit her freezing lip. "I don't like this."

He removed his weapon before easing the door open. Zac raised his gun and flashlight simultaneously, shining the beam around. He squatted and gazed into the shed from different angles before turning back to her.

"There's a wire across the threshold. Someone is trying to conceal whatever is inside. I'm calling in the team but also checking it out." He radioed for Pike to meet them and gave the location.

"But why wasn't it locked?" Olive asked.

"Perhaps they left in a hurry."

Olive tilted her head. "Shouldn't we wait for Pike and the team?"

Zac peered upward. "The storm is getting worse. We need to get inside before whoever owns this returns."

Olive approached.

"Let me go first. Avoid the wire." He stepped over the booby-trap.

The wind howled and the freezing temperatures heightened her desire to get inside. She trudged up the steps and followed his movements, gazing around the darkened room. "What type of building is this?"

Zac advanced deeper inside the long structure, away from the exit. "One of those popular portable sheds. It's raised off the ground to prevent moisture from rotting the floors."

"Interesting." Pipe bombs and wires lined a table along one wall, but stacked boxes and the darkness obstructed the remaining contents. She wanted a better look.

Olive found a light in the corner, flipped the switch, and took a step.

Click.

The noise resonated in the shed, indicating one thing.

Her action had set a deadly trap in motion.

Zac pivoted. "Don't move."

FIFTEEN

Zac's pulse hammered the moment the metallic click resonated. He'd recognize the sound anywhere. Olly had triggered a bomb installed beneath her beside the light isolated in the room's corner. He guessed the combination of stepping to the right of the shed and flipping the switch had tripped the device. Thankfully, he had been standing far enough away. But dare he move? He pressed his radio button. "Pike, report on your status to our location."

"Ten minutes out in the best of conditions, which it's not," Pike said. "Hang tight."

"Can't. Stepped on a sensor plate."

The man cursed. "How did you let that happen?"

"Not important. I need a better look at the device under the building."

"Do. Not. Move. Just in case. We're coming. Ten minutes."

"Get here fast and call for backup." Zac surmised the bomb had also triggered an alert to whoever had set it. Brad or JB? Or *was* Brad the Jingle Bell Bomber?

"Wait for us."

Like that would happen. His cell phone buzzed, and he fished it from his pocket, swiping the screen but keeping still.

I see you found my lair and triggered the bomb protecting my workshop. You have exactly 20 minutes till detonation. See if you can figure out how to disarm my intricate bomb in time. Don't listen to Pike. You can move, but tell Olly to stay perfectly still if she wants to live. JB.

Zac glanced around the room, stopping at a small camera above the doorframe. Tension knotted his muscles. JB spied on them from a safe distance.

Zac would not wait for Pike. He couldn't leave Olly exposed. It was up to him to figure out the bomb.

First, he needed a good look at what they were dealing with. To do that, he'd have to shovel a path under the shed. "Olly, this text is from JB. I can move, but you can't." He pointed to the camera. "He's watching and listening. I need to get under the shed to inspect the bomb. I'm going to

the cruiser to get my shovel. Please don't move."
He paused. "Can you do that?"

She nodded. "Please. Be. Careful."

Olly's broken words revealed her rising terror.

If only he could bring her in his arms, but that
was impossible. "Olly, stay calm. I will get you
out of this."

A tear rolled down her cheek.

He ignored the tug at his heart, stepped over
the trip wire and fled down the steps, rushing
to put on his snowshoes. He set the timer on his
watch to keep a record of every second.

He maneuvered swiftly over the snow and
hauled the shovel from the rear of the vehicle
before hastily trudging to the shed. "I'm back,"
he yelled as he kicked off his snowshoes. "Going
to shovel."

Zac thrust the tool into the snow and cleared
a small path to get under the building. Once
he felt he had enough space, he tossed it aside,
clutched his bomb kit, and crawled under to the
spot where he guessed Olly stood.

He turned and laid on his back, shining his
flashlight upward and around the exposed two-
by-four planks. JB had attached the bomb in the
corner where Olly stood, and the red blinking
light told him it was indeed armed. The digital clock read 12:01. He checked the timer on

his watch. It had taken him approximately eight minutes to get under the building.

With a little less than twelve minutes left, would Pike's team arrive on time?

Somehow, Zac doubted it. *Lord, if You were ever to hear my plea, please let it be now. Help me save Olly. She's one of Yours.*

"What's going on down there?" Olly's loud voice cracked, her emotion evident.

Zac shimmied out from under the shed and bounded up the steps. "Found the bomb. Going to disarm it."

"Is there time?"

Should he lie to keep her calm?

She would never forgive him.

"We have less than fifteen minutes." Might as well give her a ray of hope.

Her jaw dropped. "Zac, get clear of the building. Wait for Pike."

"No way. I'm going to save you. Please don't move." He bolted down the stairs and under the shed. He aimed his flashlight beam directly onto the bomb to determine if JB had installed a trip wire. He had to disarm it before proceeding. He gathered a huge breath and peered closer at the intricate assembly. Multiple wires fed up into the floor. He presumed JB had attached them to the plate and light switch.

His fingers shook not only from the cold but

from the anxiety coursing through his limbs. He had defused many bombs in his career, but not with Olly at the other end of one. He prayed for wisdom in determining the best course of action.

Minutes later, sirens sounded. Pike arrived and, for once, Zac was happy to pass the reins over to the gruff leader. Zac slid out from under the shed and sprang to his feet. He climbed the steps and entered.

Olly recited verses from the Bible. Not that he blamed her. Anything to keep her calm.

"Pike is here," he said. "I'm going to let him take over. Be right back."

She nodded and continued reciting verses.

Zac met Pike and his team at the shed's front. "So glad you're here. The bomb has less than ten minutes on it." He pointed to the foundation. "It's attached in the right corner beneath the shed."

"Stand down. We can take it from here." Pike waved his team over. "Get away from the blast zone."

"I'm staying with Olive."

"I'd advise against it, but can see the determination in your eyes."

"I don't want her to be alone during such a scary time. Don't worry, I checked the rest of the foundation and it's the only spot armed." Zac held up his phone. "Plus, JB told me I could move. The sensor plate also triggered an alert to him and there's a camera above the door. He's watching." Zac returned to the shed without waiting for a response from the man.

Olly's crumpled face told him she was losing energy fast. He needed to reassure her that help had arrived. "Pike is on it. He's got this."

"Good. Leave Zac."

"I'm not leaving you alone, Olly."

She bit her lip as her eyes darted around the room. "How did this happen?"

"JB attached multiple wires to the plate you're standing on. Once you stepped on it and flicked the light switch, you armed the device."

"Zac, my phone keeps buzzing in my pocket. Can you check to see if Grace is okay?"

He dialed Lynch's number and put her on speakerphone.

"What's up, Zac?" Lynch asked.

"We're just checking in to ensure Grace and all of you are safe."

"We're fine. Grace is coloring." Her voice warbled, telling him she'd moved away from the six-year-old. "Listen, I heard about the bomb. Olly okay?"

"Pike is working on it right now. Gotta run."

"I'm praying," Lynch said.

"Thanks. We'll touch base later." He clicked off and inserted his phone back into its holder.

Tears dripped down Olly's cheeks. "My legs hurt."

"You can't move. Any shift in weight will trigger the bomb." He longed to yank her off and take her place, but the action would kill them both. "Pike is the best in the business. He'll figure it out."

Zac prayed that was true. Sure, the man irritated everyone around him, but his vast knowledge had helped him disarm hundreds of bombs.

Right now Zac had to keep Olly's mind preoccupied and alert. Standing still in one spot, knowing she couldn't move, would heighten her tension. He realized she'd been trained in many aspects of law enforcement, but staring death in the face sometimes erased everything learned.

He searched the shed's contents and stopped at a box of small jingle bells. He walked over and scooped up a handful, raising them. "Okay, so we know this is the place where JB has been making bombs. Coincidence it's on a farmhouse belonging to Brad's family, or is your gut telling you that Brad *is* JB?" Zac required her focus to remain on the case as anything personal would only bring up past hurts.

Olly stared at the table. "I see what you're doing, Zac. Trying to keep my mind off the bomb under my feet. You must leave."

"Not happening." He let his words linger in the air. "Give me your thoughts."

She huffed. "Honestly, JB has proven himself to be too clever for that. I think he's using this place to shift the blame onto Brad. Maybe penance for his part in the school dungeon's detention room?"

Zac tapped this gloved finger on his chin. "Good point. Okay then, so where is Brad?" Once again, Zac's phone buzzed. He snatched it from his waist holder. "Text from JB." Zac read the message out loud.

You'll find Brad in his farmhouse room. He'll never hurt another child again.

The Jingle Bell Bomber was eliminating people from his past—one by one. Somehow, these victims must have influenced whatever twisted game JB played. It left Zac with one thought.

Time to stop JB before he makes another move.

Olive's legs wobbled, and she bit the inside of her bottom lip to keep herself focused on staying still.

Lord, I don't know how much longer I can hold this position. Help Pike figure out the bomb before I crumble. I don't want Zac hurt because of me.

He had shared JB's message about Brad and requested some of Pike's unit members to check the house. They awaited word on Brad's condition.

Once again, her phone buzzed. It had gone off constantly for the past five minutes. Someone desperately wanted to get in touch with her. Thankfully, Grace was fine. Who was it? She needed this to end so she could check.

"Zac, how much longer? My phone keeps buzzing."

"I'll check on the unit's progress." He pressed his radio button. "Pike, can you give me an update?"

"This bomb is definitely trickier than JB's other ones." Pike's rough voice thundered through the radio. "I reviewed the files on the way here. He's getting smarter."

Zac looked at his watch and flinched. "Time is almost up."

"Two minutes."

Olive's knees threatened to buckle, but she willed them to stay strong. In her estimation, she should have five minutes. Unless Zac hadn't given her the correct time. Not that she blamed him. She'd do the same thing, striving to give the other person hope.

"Zac, please get out. I can't let you sacrifice yourself for me." The fear in her voice was loud and clear.

His expression softened. "I told you. I'm not leaving you." He pressed the radio button again. "Pike, can you disarm it or can we switch Olive's weight with something else?"

"No can do. That only works in the movies. Trust me and let me do my job. All of our lives are at stake."

"Understood." Zac clicked off. "Sorry, he's rough around the edges."

"He's right though. I've put everyone at risk now." Heat crept up her back and resonated in her neck. "Please leave me. Tell Grace I love her."

"You can tell her yourself." He stepped forward, but stopped. "Olly, don't give up on me. You mean—"

"All clear!" Pike shouted. "Bomb disarmed."

Zac's eyes widened, and he triggered his radio. "Are you positive?"

"Yes. Bypassed JB's secondary wires. Clock stopped at thirty-five seconds."

The strength in Olive's legs depleted, and she collapsed to the floor, all adrenaline leaving her body. She sobbed as her emotions disintegrated. "I can't believe you didn't leave me."

Zac squatted and hugged her. "Shh... I've got you. You're okay."

Thank You, Lord.

Olive pushed back from his embrace. "Zac,

thank you for staying even though I told you not to. I don't know what I'd do without you."

He edged a stray strand of hair out of her eyes. "Anything for you." He stared at her lips and inched forward.

Was he going to kiss her?

Her cell phone buzzed again, reminding her of the persistent caller. "I have to check to see who this is."

He nodded and stood.

Olive inched herself into a standing position, praying her legs would hold. She fished out her phone and swiped the screen. A string of texts from her informant appeared, with the last one demanding she call him. "It's Nigel, my confidential source, and he sounds desperate." She hit the Call button.

After five rings, his voice mail kicked in. "Nigel, it's Olive. Call me when you get this."

"Odd he wasn't close to his phone since he'd been trying so hard to get in touch with you."

"I hope he's okay." She scrolled through his messages. "His text says he has information pertinent to our case. I wonder what it could be."

"Keep trying him." Zac's radio crackled.

"Turner, you have to see this," Pike said. "We're in the farmhouse."

"Let's go." Zac took Olive's arm and guided her down the steps, avoiding the booby-trap wire.

Her tired legs silently thanked him for his help.

They plodded through the snow to the side door, where officers had breached the premises. They advanced inside the abandoned farmhouse.

"Where are you, Pike?" Zac asked.

"Upstairs."

"Watch your step, Olly." Zac inched up the stairs, hugging the wall and testing each step.

Olive hesitated, not wanting to make any careless steps again. She gritted her teeth. *You can do this.* She observed Zac before matching his tippy-toed steps up to the second level, and then followed him into the room where the others had gathered. She stopped at the entrance.

Gagged, Brad had been tied to an old metal headboard. There was a knife wound to his chest. A Christmas present sat beside him with a note and a bow on the top.

Olive drew in a sharp breath. "Is there a bomb inside?"

"We checked before calling you in," Pike said. "It's clear. I'll call in Forensics and the coroner." He left the room with his team.

Fear over her earlier mistake slammed Olive in the gut again, and she cemented her feet in the entranceway. She did not want to trigger another bomb. "What's in the present?"

Zac eased the lid open and reached inside, pulling out a string of jingle bells. "Sickening."

"What does the note say?" Olive asked.

Zac unfastened it from the red bow and ribbon, turning it over. "'Brad had to pay for his sins.'"

Olive balled her fingers into fists. "We need to end this before JB kills anyone else. Odd he used a knife this time and not a bomb. Tells me he's evolving and won't stop until everyone on his supposed naughty list is wiped out."

"I hope to find his list and protect everyone on it." He walked over and handed her the note. "Same typewriter."

Olive's cell phone rang, and she snatched it up without looking at the screen. "Olive here."

"It's… Nigel." His words came out breathless.

"Nigel, what's going on?" Olive hit the speaker button. "I'm here with Constable Turner."

"Have information on JB. Get to Ottawa. Don't let him find out you're coming." His panting words sounded as if he was running.

What did that mean? Olive rubbed the bridge of her nose. "Who are you talking about?"

"Can't say. He might be listening."

"Where are you?" Zac asked.

"Come to the canal Skateway to the spot where we've met in the past, Olive. Now!" His call ended.

Zac tugged his cell phone from its holder. "I'll talk to the chief and tell him to send another team here to clear the scene. Forensics is already on its way." He checked his watch. "I think enough time has passed. I want to pick up Ziva. We need her."

They scrambled into his vehicle. Olive braced herself for another treacherous drive to Ottawa. She checked the digital dashboard's clock: 4:30. The day had passed quickly and dusk was descending upon them. They had to get to Ottawa and back in good time. The roads weren't the best in daylight, but worse after dark. She rubbed her calves to help ease the achiness. Her weary legs were on fire for holding her position for so long. *Give me strength, Lord.*

Forty-five minutes later, after picking up Ziva and facing the icy highway, Zac parked close to the canal. "Stay alert. Something or someone frightened Nigel."

They exited the cruiser.

"Now, where is the spot Nigel referred to?" Zac opened Ziva's door and she gingerly hopped down. He fastened the "Police K-9" vest onto her back. "You okay, girl?"

She barked.

Olive turned to scan the now-darkened popular Ottawa winter skating canal. Normally, it didn't open until after Christmas, but this year the weather had turned unseasonably cold in November, making it possible to start the festivities at Christmas. A rare treat that hadn't happened in years.

She pointed. "By the concession stands. I'm assuming, since you love hockey, you skate?"

"Of course, but it's been a while since I have."

"Skating is easier to get over there than walking on the ice." Olive sometimes skated on her lunch breaks during the January and February months just to think through her cases. The activity sparked her processes of working through details.

However, today was a different story. Nigel had vital information, and they required it quickly. She studied the area, but didn't see the stout fifty-year-old. Because of the weather and time of day, skaters were scarce. A man in an orange vest and winter mask worked at the rink's edge on the Zamboni-like machine's engine. Normally, the ice resurfacer was deployed at night, but the man tinkering with it must be fixing it to give the Skateway maintenance team an early start due to the weather.

"I don't see him yet, but let's go." Olive led Zac and Ziva over to the booth where they rented skates in their sizes. After lacing up, they skated to the concession stands where a bench sat on the ice. Music blared through nearby speakers, and she cringed as "Jingle Bells" blasted. Did they have to play that song?

Ziva stayed close to Zac, struggling to walk on the slippery surface.

Olive checked the time on her cell phone. "He

should be here by now. I'm worried. He seemed skittish on the phone."

"Where did you find this informant?"

Olive eased herself down onto the bench. "Believe it or not, he found me. I'd been investigating a high-profile case, and a newspaper article included my name. He called because he said he had more information I needed to hear. He helped us create a more accurate profile, and we apprehended the suspect."

"So, you've been working with him ever since?"

"Yes, but he's never been this nervous before." Olive scanned the depleting crowd. The resurfacer had maneuvered onto the rink, driving slowly. Obviously, the worker had fixed the issue.

"I'm here," a raspy voice said from behind their position.

Olive stood and pivoted, her skate catching a crack in the ice. She wavered.

Zac caught her by the waist and steadied her. "Got you."

Olive freed herself of Zac's hold, ignoring the sudden flush in her cheeks. "Nigel, you scared me. I expected you to come from the other direction."

"Sorry. I wanted to watch from behind the trees just to be sure you weren't followed." Nigel skated around the bench and stuck out his hand to Zac. "Nigel."

Zac shook his hand. "Constable Zac Turner." He gestured to his dog. "This is Ziva."

"She's beautiful." He inspected the area before turning to Olive. "Let's make this quick."

Olive grabbed his arm. "Are you being followed? I've never seen you so skittish before."

Zac and Olive sat back down, Ziva at their side. "He knows I know."

The music's volume increased, making it difficult to hear.

"Who and what are you talking about?" Zac asked. "And how did you learn all this being in Ottawa?"

"I have contacts all over the province, including Stittsrock Falls." He leaned closer. "I don't know the man's name, but I've heard he's good at tapping into people's devices, so beware."

Like they didn't already realize that.

The snowfall intensified. Time to move. "What information do you have?"

Nigel shifted his stance, but his skate slipped and he stumbled backward before catching himself. "JB's mother's identity. She was wrongly convicted—"

An engine roared behind them.

Ziva barked.

The resurfacing machine careened along the icy surface, heading directly for Nigel. The loud music had hid its approach.

Another worker dressed in a matching orange vest ran onto the rink, flailing his arms.

Olive and Zac bolted upward.

"Nigel, get out of the way!" Zac lurched forward, but his words were too late.

The resurfacer had barreled over Nigel before racing down the ice.

Olive skated to Nigel, dropping to her knees too quickly and hitting her elbow hard. She clutched her arm and slid over to Nigel. She felt for a pulse, but found none. The impact of the one-thousand-gallon, water-filled machine had killed him instantly.

JB had targeted her CI before he could provide any information that might help them finally identify the Jingle Bell Bomber.

SIXTEEN

"**O**fficer in need of assistance. Send units and EMS!" Zac yelled into his radio, giving them their location. He observed Nigel. The man lay on his back, lifeless eyes lifted toward the snowy sky. Zac guessed the driver had intentionally hit Olly's CI, but who was the other worker heading toward them?

Olly cried out.

"No!" Zac yelled, crouch-sliding across the ice to where she lay. "Olly! What happened?"

"Fell hard on my arm." Her lip trembled. "Nigel's gone."

Ziva skidded over to Olly and nudged herself tight to her as if protecting her new friend.

The masked worker approached. "You guys okay?"

"Why was your machine out on the ice while skaters were around?" Zac's stern tone revealed his frustration.

The man threw his hands up. "No idea. It wasn't

supposed to be, and he's not one of our workers. That's why I was trying to get to the machine."

Zac glanced down the ice to where the resurfacer had fled. The machine stood abandoned several yards away. The driver was nowhere to be seen. Had JB somehow gotten access to it to take out Nigel?

"I gotta get in touch with my boss. We have to write this incident up." The man shuffled toward the machine, shaking his head.

A growing number of skaters watched from a distance. Seemed the resurfacer's fatal hit had drawn their attention.

A younger man skated toward them at rapid speed.

Zac placed his hand on his Glock, ready to take action.

The man raised his hands. "I'm a doctor. How can I help?"

Zac loosened his hand at his side and gestured toward Nigel. "The machine hit him hard."

The doctor knelt and checked his vitals. "I'm afraid he's gone."

"Olly hurt her arm. Can you check on her? EMS is on their way, but I'm not sure how far out they are." Zac brushed snow off his jacket. "I'm Constable Turner. You are?"

"Doctor Rankin." He moved over to Olly. "Let me look."

Sirens pierced the air, announcing emergency services. *Thank you.* Zac didn't want to leave Olly's side to look for the suspect. Just in case the driver, who Zac suspected to be JB, waited to once again pounce. He couldn't risk her life. *Wow, what a day this has been.* First Olly stepped on a bomb and now this. When would it end?

Not until they caught the Jingle Bell Bomber. But JB had taken out Nigel before he been able to give them all the information he'd had. The only thing he'd said was JB's mother was wrongly convicted, leaving a question floating in Zac's mind.

Convicted of what? That could have been lots of cases in Ontario. Most suspects claimed to be innocent, so how was this one different?

Olly winced, bringing him back to the situation.

Dr. Rankin had removed her arm from her coat, inspecting it. "Sorry. I know it hurts, but it appears you hit your elbow hard. It's starting to swell. It will require ice, but you'll be okay. Someone was looking out after you, ma'am." He helped her sit up.

Was that true? If so, why had God allowed others to die? Why allow evil at all?

It was a question that had bothered Zac for years now. His thoughts turned to his father and the crimes he had committed throughout his mob years. There were too many to count.

Shouts alerted Zac to others joining the scene.

Police officers carefully made their way over the ice to the group, approaching Zac.

"Constable Bracken," Olly said. "Why are you here?"

"Boss reassigned me after the bombing at the federal building." The man's eyes shifted to the motionless CI on the rink. "What happened?"

Zac pointed. "Ice resurfacer barreled into Nigel, but the driver fled in that direction. Can you and your men scour the area to see if you can find him and clear the scene? JB is good, so check everywhere."

"On it. Olive, take care and stay safe." Bracken turned to the others. "Let's go."

Zac resisted the urge to let the anger rising overtake his emotions. He'd almost lost Olly and Ziva. Again.

JB, this has to stop.

His phone buzzed and he checked the screen. *Mom. Sorry, I don't have time to chat right now.* He hated to ignore her, but Olly was his top priority at the moment. He clicked Decline. *I'll call you later. I promise.*

Their relationship had been strained ever since he'd found out about the secret she'd kept from him. However, he longed for the closeness they'd once held.

Forgive her. She was only protecting you, like you are Olly.

Was that true?

"Zac, help them secure the scene," Olly said. "I'll be okay here with Ziva."

Olly's statement not only surprised him, but tore him from his thoughts. The fact that Ziva made her feel safe warmed his heart. "Doc, can you stay with her? After we ensure everyone is safe, the paramedics can step in."

The man nodded.

"Ziva, stay." Zac skated to the remaining skaters and asked if they'd seen anything, specifically the driver's face. But none had.

After Constable Bracken and his team reassured Zac the driver was indeed gone, Zac waved in the paramedics. They checked Olly over and put her arm in a sling, instructing her to ice it when she returned home.

Home?

Three hours later, after fixing the group spaghetti for a late night supper and ensuring Olly rested comfortably, Zac sat at the dining room table in front of his laptop. He wanted to research cases where a woman had been allegedly wrongfully convicted.

Constable Bracken had contacted him to let him know that, after a thorough investigation into the incident, the only evidence he'd found was a discarded Stittsrock Falls police uniform. The driver had escaped posing as a constable.

The news sent Zac's anxiety skyrocketing. Somehow JB had secured the clothing under their noses. How had he accessed their police station?

Zac hit Enter on his keyboard and waited. Within seconds, multiple hits appeared on his screen. Too many for him to search through by himself. He would get the others at the station to help tomorrow.

The floor creaked behind him.

He pivoted, senses on high alert.

Olly shuffled forward and plunked herself in the chair beside him. "Sorry, didn't mean to scare you."

"Why are you up?"

"Couldn't sleep. My elbow is okay, but I keep thinking about Nigel." Tears rolled down her cheeks. "He died trying to help me. I'm responsible for his death."

Zac rubbed a tear away, letting his thumb linger on her chin. "Don't say that. The driver was. No one else."

She cupped her hand over his and held it on her face. "Thank you for saying that. You're a good friend."

He stared at her mouth, the desire for more than friends wavering his resolve to stay out of a relationship. But being around her the past few days had chipped at the ice wall he'd constructed around his heart.

Their gaze held.

Stay strong. Remember.

The thought pushed him to his feet. He walked to the window and stared into the backyard, not wanting to see the disappointment he guessed was on her face. "I'm on a later shift tomorrow, so I'll head in to the station. I want to get everyone's help in sifting through cases of a woman claiming her innocence." He turned.

Olly had disappeared as quickly and quietly as she'd appeared.

Zac fisted his hands. He had done it again. Raised her hopes and shattered them all within a minute.

Olive woke to a thump in the room she shared with her foster child, followed by the pitter-patter of feet.

"Mommy, only three days till Santa comes!" Grace bounced on the bed before she tugged on Olive's arm. "Get up. I want to build a snowman."

Olive winced, holding a breath to let the pain subside while processing the fact that Grace had called her "Mommy." Warmth coursed through her weary body. She had longed to hear someone call her Mommy ever since she'd lost the child she'd been carrying. The pain had numbed her, sending her through the motions of life, carrying a gaping hole in her chest—an invisible scarlet letter of sorts, branding her wounded heart with a mark hidden to everyone around her. It had not only crushed her, but instilled her fear of ever getting pregnant again. She could not go through the pain of losing another child.

She sat up and hugged the little girl beside her, holding her close. Olive had finally heard back from her lawyer, stating he'd sent in the papers. *Lord, please let the courts approve Grace's adoption.* "Sweetie, we still have lots to do before Santa arrives, but right now, Mommy has to rest."

Grace's face twisted in a disgruntled expression. "But you've been sleeping too long."

Olive peered at the clock.

How could it already be one in the afternoon? Yesterday's events must have conked her out after she'd returned from the awkward conversation with Zac. She had left when he had his back turned, not wanting him to see her disappointment all over again.

She threw back the covers. "You're right, Ladybug. Time to get up."

"Yay!" Grace scrambled off the bed and out of the room, singing "Jingle Bells."

If she only realized the song's impact right now.

Olive picked up her cell phone and brought it to life. She had set it to Do Not Disturb at Zac's request—no, at his order. Olive noticed she'd missed multiple messages and texts. She checked the number.

Her father.

Olive stood quickly. White spots flickered in her vision and she teetered. She held on to the headboard to steady herself. *Stupid, Olly.* She should know better than to pounce out of bed after an injury.

But something told her Carson Wells required her attention. He hadn't called her in months after their fight over her mother's care. She clicked the most recent message and listened.

"Olly, I'm not sure why you're not picking up, but your mother needs you. She's frantic. Something about jingle bells. She won't settle. Call me." Her father's agitated voice and the words *jingle bells* raised her guard.

Olive dressed quickly in jeans and a Christmas plaid shirt. No time for her normal work clothes. She scurried from the room as fast as her weary body allowed.

She stopped at Zac's closed door and pounded. "Zac, are you in there?" She remembered him telling her about his later shift, but had he left without her?

Seconds later, the door opened and a sleepy Zac stood wearing a T-shirt, pajama bottoms, and bare feet. "What's wrong?"

She ignored the urge to stare at his muscular

biceps and raised her cell phone. "My dad called multiple times. Something about Mom and jingle bells. Do you know if anything has happened at Stittsrock Falls Manor?"

His eyes widened. "I silenced my cell phone after our long, hard shift. Let me check." He snatched his phone from the nightstand and swiped the screen. "Oh, no."

"What is it? Is my mom okay?"

He held up the phone. "Text from JB, only sent to me."

I left Olly's Mom a note along with her Christmas present. The game is almost over. JB.

Olive's knees buckled and she sank to the floor. "No! He can't take my mom."

"He won't. I'm calling Pike right now. Get ready. We're leaving." He helped her stand before hitting a number on his phone.

Olive's eyes watered and she rubbed them to stop the tears. *Stay strong.* She fumbled to put her coat and boots on as her pulse spiked at the thought of the Jingle Bell Bomber killing her precious mother.

Lord protect Mama.

Zac steered his cruiser into Stittsrock Falls Manor, siren blaring. He had relayed the information to Chief Bennett, who had assured him he would get Pike and his unit there as fast as possible. However, Zac wanted Ziva there faster. Her detector skills were quicker than Pike's, even though the man wouldn't admit to the fact. The chief had requested the building be cleared, but Zac knew that would take time. Time they didn't have.

Olly had remained silent on the trip to her mother's nursing home, chewing constantly on her hair.

He killed the engine and turned to her. "Pike will arrive any minute, but I want Ziva to search the building first. You stay here."

She snapped out of her trance, dropping her hair and opening the door. "Not happening." She bounded toward the one-level nursing home.

"Ugh!" Zac jumped from the vehicle, unleashing Ziva. "Come."

The pair headed to the door and Zac tugged it open. "Ziva, seek."

His partner limped down a long corridor, her claws clicking on the floor.

Zac noted Olly running into a room.

A nurse stopped him before he could follow. "What's the meaning of this?"

"Ma'am, please get everyone out of the building." Zac hated to yell at the woman, but she needed to be aware of the situation's urgency. "Didn't my chief call?"

"Yes, but an evacuation takes time in a nursing home. The manor's owner is organizing it right now." The petite nurse latched onto his arm. "Is it a bomb?"

"Undetermined."

Sirens blared as Pike's unit parked under the canopy at the building's entrance.

"Get everyone out. Now!" He unhooked his radio. "Pike, Ziva is tracking. Will update soon."

Somewhere down the hall, Ziva barked. Not her normal alert, but she obviously wanted her partner fast.

Zac didn't wait for a response, but sprinted toward his K-9's call. "Ziva, where are you?"

Another bark directed him into the room across the hall from where Olly had entered.

Ziva sat beside an elderly man's bed.

The bomb was close by.

"What's the meaning of this?" The man's gruff voice revealed trepidation.

Zac ignored him for now and knelt beside his Lab. "Good girl." Zac peeked under the bed.

A Christmas present lay within reach.

Zac bolted upright. "Sir, we need you to evacuate. Can you walk?"

The man harrumphed and stood. "Of course I can. Do you think I'm frail or something?"

Ouch. Zac didn't have time to argue. "Can you grab your coat and find a nurse? Please leave the building."

"I know what's going on. I read the papers." He pointed a knobby finger at Ziva. "That's a detector dog, isn't it?"

"She is."

"I used to be a judge and I'm familiar with law enforcement." He took his coat from the closet. "Don't worry, I'm leaving." He shuffled from the room.

A judge? Is that why JB targeted this man's room?

Zac ignored his unspoken question and pressed the talk button on his radio. "Pike, bomb located. Under the bed in wing C, room 135."

"Got it, Turner. Stand down."

Zac didn't listen and turned to his partner. "Ziva, seek." Zac motioned for his K-9 to search the entire floor. He'd learned from experience, there could be more.

She understood his command and raced out of the room.

Zac stepped inside Mrs. Wells's room.

Olly sat beside her mother's rocking chair, struggling to get the frazzled woman's arm through her coat sleeve. "Mama. We have to leave."

The woman raised a bony finger toward the desk. "Jingle bells."

Zac followed the woman's attention to a poinsettia. A tiny note positioned in the cardette held jingle bells dangling from a ribbon. "I'll get it, Olly. We need to get out. Found the package. Ziva is searching for others."

Olly's jaw dropped, but she held in any other reaction. Obviously, for her mother's sake.

Zac picked up the note and read it.

Mrs. Wells,

I'm a friend of your daughter's and wanted to send you a gift.

Merry Christmas. JB

The *J* was missing the bottom loop, confirming the card had been typed on the same typewriter as all the others.

The Jingle Bell Bomber had targeted Olly's mother.

Zac had to get Evelyn Wells and her daughter out of the building.

Olive held her mother's hand two hours later and struggled to hold in her tears. This latest threat had hit too close to home. To target Olive was one thing, but now he'd victimized her mother? That was an entirely different story. Olive balled her free hand into a fist, her determination to catch JB intensifying. Thankfully, Ziva had cleared the rest of the manor building and Pike's team had quickly disarmed the bomb without detonation. *Thank You, Lord.*

Zac and Ziva stood guard in the door's entrance. His stoic expression revealed he also wanted the game resolved.

The team had once again gathered at the station to go through cases. Olive and Zac would join them as soon as Olive had calmed her mother's frantic state.

Carson Wells sat on his wife's bedside, cradling his head in his hands. "How could you let this happen, Olly?"

How dare you accuse me, Dad. Words she wanted to say, but she bit her tongue. "This isn't my fault. This maniac is targeting my family."

He jumped off the bed. "Time to quit your job. You almost killed your mother."

Zac stepped closer. "Sir, with all due respect, that's not true. Without your daughter's help, we wouldn't have gotten this far. She's good at what she does."

Olive kissed her mother's forehead. "Mama, it's gonna be okay. You're safe."

Evelyn Wells's tears finally subsided, and she patted Olive's hand. "It's bath time, Olly. Don't forget to wash behind your ears."

The woman's trepidation had disappeared at the snap of a finger, taking her back to Olive's childhood. That's what it was now like with her mother's condition.

"Okay, Mama. I'll get the nurse." Olive walked to her father. "Don't chastise me. I love you, Dad, but this isn't my fault." She refused to give him the satisfaction of a tantrum. Olive turned to Zac. "Thank you, but I can fight my own battles." She bent to kiss Ziva's head. "Thanks, girl, for saving my mother."

She left the room in search of a nurse, regretting her harshness to Zac, but her earlier panic had caught up to her and she hadn't been able to help herself. *I'm sorry, Lord. Will I ever be more like You?*

The drive to the station after settling her mother reeked with nasty silence. She hated herself for her harshness and knew she must apologize. He hadn't deserved her wrath.

She reached across the console and squeezed his shoulder. "I'm sorry for getting angry with you too. Blame it on pent-up frustration over my strained relationship with Dad and my terror of almost losing my mother to a bomb. Can you forgive me?"

He turned, a gorgeous smile crinkling the lines beside his eyes. "I didn't mean to get in the middle. I understand. Mom and I aren't what you'd call close right now either."

She pulled back. "What? Why? You were always inseparable."

His expression clouded. "How's your arm?"

She studied his face. "Zac, what aren't you telling me?"

He drove into the station's lot and parked next to an ambulance. "That doesn't look good. Come on." Zac gathered Ziva from her cage.

Olive followed them into the building, and Griff greeted them. "What's going on?" she asked.

"Bomb in the chief's office." Griff turned to Zac. "He's okay, but they're asking for you. Seems JB left you a message."

Her heartbeat thudded as a question invaded Olive's mind.

How would JB's game end?

SEVENTEEN

Zac hustled down the hall toward the chief's office, praying his boss hadn't been hurt. Footsteps told him Olly had followed. Once again, this deadly bomber had somehow infiltrated his gifts into their lives. What had it cost this time? He turned the corner and stumbled into the disarrayed office.

Brett stood beside the chief, inspecting Bennett's eyes.

Pike lifted his gaze from analyzing the charred gift when Zac entered the room. "A gift left on the chief's desk just exploded, but it was contained. It obviously was meant only to scare this time around and not kill."

Olly appeared at the entrance. "How did someone get by everyone to plant the gift?"

Zac rubbed his temples. "Good question. Let's check our video footage." He turned to the chief. "Chief, you okay?"

The man mumbled. "Ticked JB got the drop

on me. I came in from getting a coffee and the gift was on my desk. The note on top said 'From your staff,' so I didn't even think twice when I lifted the lid."

"The truck delivered our annual Christmas toys for the kids and we checked them all before bringing them into the station. Not sure how this one landed on Bennett's desk." Pike handed Zac the charred box lid. "This low-impact bomb wasn't meant to kill. Not sure why."

"He's telling us he's in charge, not the chief." Olly walked up to the trio. "Where's the note?"

Pike pointed. "Check the lid, Turner. It survived because the inside didn't blow until after the chief removed it."

Zac read the typewritten message out loud. "'Zac, buddy, the game is almost over. Stop your investigation or next time the chief will die.'"

He handed it to Olly. "Like that's gonna happen. If the game is almost over, who's left on his naughty list?"

Olly looked at the note. "Wait, he called you 'buddy.' Has he done that before?"

"No. What do you think it means?"

"JB is someone close to you, Zac."

Zac sucked in a fragmented breath. "No one I know would do something like this. I want to check the video footage. Now." He addressed

Bennett. "Get to the hospital. We've got this. Brett, take good care of him."

"I will." Brett pulled Zac aside. "I need to talk to you."

"What's up?"

The paramedic's shoulders sagged. "My dad was just diagnosed with cancer. I'm heading out west to my hometown tomorrow to check on him."

Zac squeezed his friend's arm. "I'm so sorry. I'll be praying."

"Thanks. Let's hope God listens to you." Brett turned back to the chief. "Let's go."

They left.

Five minutes later, Olly and Zac sat in the situation room ready to check the footage, but Jacqueline, the cleaner, was busy vacuuming the floor.

Zac snapped his fingers to get her attention. "Jacqueline, sorry, but can you do this later? We need the space." Why was she always in the way?

She pursed her lips but turned off the vacuum. She brushed by Griff as he entered the room.

Griff plunked a stack of files in front of them. "These are all the cases of a woman claiming to be innocent within the past five years you requested." He motioned air quotes around *innocent*.

"Wait, why aren't we looking online?" Zac opened a folder.

"Because our system is down at the moment. We had a power outage a couple of hours ago, but it's fixed now. After it came back on, we realized a virus had wiped our system. Odd timing, don't you think?" Griff walked to the door. "Good thing the chief is old school and had printed the files. I'll get the others. This calls for all hands on deck."

Olly gathered an inch of files from the stack. "We must identify JB. This woman has to be the key."

Thankfully, they had a large pot of coffee. Zac stood and poured himself a cup. "Let's check the footage first. Perhaps whoever caused the power outage also planted the gift in Bennett's office. Hopefully, the videos weren't wiped out with the virus." He sat back down and clicked a file.

An image appeared on the monitor. "Good. Here we go. I'll take it back a bit." He hit Rewind.

"Wait. Stop there." Olly pointed.

Zac stopped the footage and pressed Play. A dark image of a masked individual entering through the back entrance appeared. He limped forward. "This has to be our suspect. The boot imprints revealed a limp."

Seconds later, the screen went snowy.

"No!" Zac fast-forwarded, but the rest of the surveillance was gone. He huffed and slouched. "He erased them somehow. This guy is good."

"Do you know anyone that technical?"

"Almost everyone." His cell phone buzzed and he checked this screen. His mother. *Sorry, Mom. I don't have time for you today.* He hit Decline. "Let's look through these folders."

Griff returned, along with two other officers. They all poured a coffee before sitting at the table and snagging a stack of folders.

Olly's phone rang. "It's Lauren." She hit a button. "Hi, Lauren. You're on speaker with Zac, Griff and the team. Everything okay at the house?"

"Yes, they're outside building a snowman. I have news. I've been looking through Pastor Felix's records. Thankfully, Forensics retrieved them after obtaining the warrant. The pastor had digitized everything, including his calendar."

Zac tensed. "What did you find?"

"Repetitive appointments in his calendar with the initials DP."

"But why is that odd?" Griff asked.

"Because all his other appointments have full names. It looks like he kept this one a secret. It could be nothing, but we always suspected there was some type of connection between the church and the first couple of victims. Maybe this is it."

"Interesting," Olly said. "Good work, Lauren."

"Just thought it might be important. I'll let you know if I find anything else." She clicked off.

"Let's keep that information in the back of our minds." Zac picked up a file. "Time to start on this mountain of paperwork."

An hour later, Zac sagged in his chair, rubbing his weary eyes. "So far, I've found nothing remotely suspicious." He glanced at the team. "Have any of you?"

Griff slammed a folder shut. "Nothing. Just the same thing over and over. Victims claimed they were innocent, but then confessed."

Olly gasped. "Wait. This one is interesting. A woman claimed to be innocent even after being convicted of her sister's death."

Zac leaned forward. "What happened to her?"

"She hung herself on—" Olly's gaze flipped to his.

Zac sensed a light bulb just flashed in Olly's brain. "On?"

"Christmas Day."

Silence paused the room.

"She must be the one Nigel referred to," Olly said.

"What was her name?" Zac asked.

"Darla Parsons." Olly's eyes bulged. "DP. Could this be the person Pastor Felix had been meeting with?"

"And why he was killed." Zac sprang out of his chair. "This has to be JB's mother. Somehow, he blamed the pastor and the rest of our victims. Let's look into this case closer."

Zac exhaled.

Finally, the break they'd needed.

Olive's angst matched the rhythm of Zac's fingers drumming on the table as they waited for Griff to display the case details on the monitor. They had secured the files from a station just outside of Stittsrock Falls in the town where Darla's trial had been held.

Olive had videoed in Lauren to let her know what they'd found. Her pretty face appeared on Olive's tablet as they all waited. The anticipation of putting the jigsaw pieces together of this puzzling case hung heavy in the air.

Zac's cell phone buzzed. He scowled and turned his phone over.

Olive placed her hand on top of his. "Everything okay?"

"My mom keeps calling, but I don't have time right now. This case is important." He rubbed her hand with his thumb. "We're so close to cracking it."

"Maybe you should call her while we wait. She might—"

"Got it," Griff said. "Here we go."

The case details displayed in full view, interrupting Olive's plea for Zac to call his mother.

Zac stood and walked closer. "Okay. Darla Parsons, age fifty-six, arrested twenty-four months ago on December 25 for allegedly killing her sister who was in her care. She denied it, stating it was an accident."

"Wait. She was arrested on Christmas Day?" Griff asked.

"Yes, and later convicted after a jury all voted her guilty." Zac folded his arms and kept reading. "Then, after serving a few more months in jail, she hung herself on Christmas Day one year ago."

Olive hopped up from her chair. "That's JB's trigger. She has to be his mother."

Zac pointed to Griff. "Check her records for the son's name."

"On it." Griff typed on his laptop.

Olive paced, thinking about the victims, and paused. "Wait, what was the trial judge's name?"

"I'm checking," Lauren said. "Here it is. Jacob Walters."

Olive focused on Lauren. "Walters, you said?"

"Yes, why?"

Olive turned to Zac. "That's the older gentleman targeted across the hall in Mom's nursing home. He just retired because of Alzheimer's and was admitted to Mom's special wing."

Zac advanced the screen to the report's next

page. "The arresting officer was Constable Jack Everett."

"This case sounds familiar. Just a sec." Lauren clicked on her keyboard. "I knew it. I remember Rick talking about her trial. He provided the Forensic evidence."

Olive whirled around. "And what do you want to guess Mary Jones was on the jury that convicted her?"

Zac placed his hands on the table, leaning into the group. "This is it. Let's check everyone else involved in that trial. Jury. Lawyers. Police. Everyone. That's how JB has chosen his naughty list. We have to stop him before he continues."

"Didn't he say the game was almost over?" Olive asked. "Who's left? Us?"

Griff slammed his palm down. "You're kidding me!"

"What is it?" Zac asked.

"Darla Parsons had a son, but his name is not on any records." Griff turned his laptop around. "Here's the birth certificate."

Olive inched closer for a better view.

The child's name had been redacted. How was that possible? The year of birth, though, was still visible.

Olive froze. "Zac, I'm thinking we went to high school with the son. Look at the year he was born."

Zac eyed the screen. "Possibly."

Brynn charged into the room. "Zac, your mother is on the phone. She says it's urgent she speak with you."

Zac punched the phone's button. "Mom, you're on speaker. What's going on?"

"Help! Zac, he's in the house. He found us." A crash sounded in the background and the call dropped.

Olive studied Zac's blanched face. The call had changed his demeanor in an instant.

Whoever *he* was, clearly had Zac rattled.

Zac and the Stittsrock Falls' Emergency Response Unit huddled around the tactical armored vehicle down the street from his mother's home, hidden from his father's view. They were all in full gear. Ziva sat by his side, ready for action and equipped with a Kevlar vest. Zac wanted her protected at all times.

He had tasked Griff to look into Darla Parsons's case closer. Zac did not want the case to suffer because of his father's sudden appearance. Olly had insisted she come, but he'd made her promise she'd stay inside the vehicle when the ERU moved in. For now, she stood waiting with the group for Zac's instructions.

Brett's ambulance was parked to the team's right, just in case they were needed.

"Listen up," Zac said. "Harry Burns will have at least four heavily armed men stationed around the perimeter. We need to subdue them before entering the house."

The ERU captain grabbed his arm. "Are you talking about the infamous British Columbia mob boss, Harry Burns?"

"Yes. The one and only."

"Why would he be in your mother's house, Zac?" Olly asked.

Zac stole a glimpse at his ex-fiancée. *Here we go. The moment of truth.* Now she'll really hate him, but he had to share all the details with this unit. He refused to put them at risk.

He suppressed a sigh. "Because Harry Burns is my father. He's here to take revenge on my mother for moving us to Ontario and changing our identities."

"What?" Olly toppled backward.

He caught her before she fell. "I'll explain everything later," he whispered.

She scowled and climbed into the armored vehicle.

Obviously distancing herself from him. His secret had been exposed and now he'd pay the price for keeping it from her for so long. Would she forgive him?

He set the thought aside and turned back to the team. "These men are ruthless. They've killed many during their money laundering years. Please, save my mother." He paused, composing himself. "You all have your assignments. Let's do this."

Each man nodded and broke to get into position. Not being trained with the team, Zac and Ziva stayed behind, waiting for the all-clear that they'd subdued his father's men.

That seemed like an eternity, but ten minutes later, the team captain gave the go-ahead for Zac to follow the officers into his mother's house. He knew she'd be petrified, so he'd insisted he and Ziva enter at the same time.

Zac skulked behind the unit, crouch-walking. He had his Glock ready to fire, if required. They approached the side door in stealth mode and Zac passed the captain his key.

The captain gave the signal and silently opened the door. The unit pressed forward, each taking a different route through the home.

Beside him, Ziva became agitated and growled. Zac struggled to keep his partner by his side.

This was not her typical alert response.

Something was off.

"Hurry," Zac whispered into his com unit. "Ziva has alerted to danger."

They inched closer to the living room just as his mother screamed.

The captain raised a fisted hand, indicating everyone to hold position. "Zac, release your partner," he said through the mic. "The element of surprise will knock the attention away from your mother. We'll be right behind Ziva."

God, if You're listening. I need You. Protect Mom and Ziva. I can't lose either. I promise I'll come back to You.

Zac inhaled and unfastened Ziva's leash. "Ziva, go."

His partner bolted into the living room as quick as her sprained leg would allow.

Zac and the team followed the K-9.

Harry Burns had a gun pointed at his mother.

A man off to the side turned and raised his weapon, finger depressing the trigger.

The ERU captain fired, and the man dropped.

The normally docile Ziva leaped over a chair and positioned herself in front of Harry, barking and baring her teeth. Her expression revealed her intent and was enough of an intimidating distraction to surprise his father.

The unit advanced and subdued the mob boss.

"Ziva, out!" Zac yelled.

Ziva backed away and ceased her barking.

Zac rushed over to his mother and untied her hands, bringing her into an embrace. "I've got you, Mom. You're okay. Ziva saved you."

His mother crumpled in Zac's arms, sobbing.

"So, this is my son," Burns said. "A cop. Figures." He struggled in the captain's hold. "This is not over, *son*."

His emphasis on the word son sent shivers hurtling throughout Zac's body. *Lord, help his conviction stick this time.*

"Mr. Burns, you're going away for a long time." The captain shoved a cuffed Harry toward the door. "Time to visit your new home." He turned back to Zac. "I'll send the paramedics in to check your mother."

Zac nodded and hugged his mother tighter. "I'm so sorry for not calling you back. The case I'm working on has taken up all my time."

"I wanted to tell you I'd felt like someone was following me."

Zac inwardly chastised himself for not paying attention to his mother's calls and texts. "I'm so sorry. I would never have forgiven myself if something had happened."

"I had to break my silence and call your station. I saw Harry from the downstairs window just before his men broke into the house."

Brett and his partner burst through the doors, followed by Olly.

She scurried to his mother's side and squatted. "Abby, are you okay?"

Abigail Turner cupped her palm on Olly's right cheek. "Dear, it's so nice to see you. What are you doing here?"

"Mom, Olly has been helping with the case I referred to earlier."

Olly fisted her hands on her hips. "Zac Turner, you have some explaining to do. Tell me what's going on."

"Zac, honey, it's time to tell Olly the truth."

"I know. Later, at the house. Mom, you'll be staying with us for a bit. There's lots of room."

He must protect the three women in his life he loved. His mother, Olly, and Ziva.

What? He just admitted to himself he still loved Olive Wells. The question was…

Would she hate him now that she had discovered the secret he'd kept from her?

Olive waited by the fireplace for Zac to return. Ziva lay curled on a mat close by. Brett had cleared Abby of any injuries, and she'd packed a bag before heading with them to the safe house. Harry Burns would be held in Stittsrock Falls until his charges were determined. Until that time, Zac had said he wanted his mother at his side. She now slept in the bedroom across from Olive's.

Olive had tucked a tired Grace into bed and read her favorite Christmas story. She had fallen asleep before Olive got to the book's middle. Seemed building a snowman was hard work. She chuckled, even though she was not in a joyful mood. Zac had lied to her. Keeping a secret this important was hard to come back from.

But you also hold a secret.

The thought passed through her mind so quickly she almost missed it. She rested her hand on her abdomen. A natural reaction whenever she thought of her closet skeleton.

Zac's voice alerted her to his presence. "Thanks for the update." He clicked off his cell phone and sat in the rocker on the other side of the fireplace. "That was Griff. He discovered an old deed to Darla Parsons's home. Seems like it was never sold. He staked it out, and it appears someone still lives there. We're getting a search warrant, so hopefully the judge will sign it by morning. We're close to finding out JB's identity. Right now, Griff and Skye are out on a date."

Ziva's ears had perked up at her handler's appearance.

He reached down and petted her. "Good girl."

"Really? I didn't realize they were dating."

"This is their first." Zac stared into the rising embers, growing silent. "Just hope it doesn't ruin their working relationship."

"Why did you lie to me about your identity?" Olive didn't hold back the irritation from her voice.

"Because I had to protect you from him." Zac's gaze switched to hers and held. "I found out six months after we were engaged that my mother was married to a monster who vowed revenge on her and me for leaving him. She'd kept this from me all of my life. I was two, so I barely remember him."

"So, that's the real reason you ended our engagement?"

"Yes."

She broke their locked gaze and stared at the floor. "I would have kept your secret, Zac."

"Olly, I couldn't risk him finding me and taking his revenge out on you. I loved you that much." He got up and squatted in front of her, taking her hands in his. "Do you realize how much it broke my heart to leave? You were my everything."

She couldn't go there right now. "What's your real name?"

"Devin Burns."

She pulled back. "Doesn't suit you."

"I will keep Zac Turner since Mom changed it legally." He picked up the poker and stirred the fire. "Can you ever forgive me?"

"I don't know, Zac." God commanded His children to forgive like He forgave them, but could she?

He placed the poker back and brought her to her feet. "I'm sorry." He caressed her face.

"I'm not sure I can come back from the secret." She recognized deep down that was not the reason. Absently, she clutched her tummy. She couldn't commit to any relationship. The pain still held her in a vise after many years. When would she be able to let go?

He huffed, raising a brow. "You have secrets of your own, don't you? Tell me."

"Zac, it's been a long day. Can we talk about it later?" *Why stall? Confess, Olly. He deserves the truth.* She averted her eyes away from the man she knew she still loved.

He let out a long exhale. "I'm going to take some time to scour the perimeter. G'night, Olly." He addressed his partner. "Ziva, come." The two departed the living room.

Moments later, the front door opened and closed, telling Olive they had left.

She stared at the fireplace as the embers danced, flickering light into the darkened room in syncopation with the twinkling Christmas tree decorations. She wasn't sure how long she sat there until the back door closed softly again. *Time for bed, Olive.*

After changing into pajamas, she kissed Grace's forehead before getting into bed, the day's happenings still fresh on her mind. She struggled to contain them as excitement rose.

Thoughts of closing the JB Bomber case eased her agitation, and she shut her eyes.

A hand clasped over her mouth just as a needle pricked her neck. She opened her eyes and gazed at the Jingle Bell Bomber's face.

Her world faded to black as his identity flashed in her mind.

EIGHTEEN

Zac shuffled from his room, carrying his laptop early the next morning, in need of a strong coffee. His restless sleep had robbed him of strength and he required a caffeine kick. He walked to Olly's closed door at the back of the house and stopped. He checked his watch. Odd. For the past few days since she's been back in his life, she was normally up before him. Perhaps yesterday's events and his exposed secret identity had also stolen her strength. He'd let her sleep. For now, he wanted to check on the search warrant status. *Lord, help the judge sign off on it. Thank You for saving us all yesterday.* Zac hadn't forgotten the promise he made to God, but right now his thoughts returned to the case.

He moved into the kitchen and brewed a strong pot of his favorite coffee for the team. While waiting, he turned on his laptop and signed into his account.

Ziva trotted into the kitchen, nudging her nose on Zac's leg.

"You're walking better already, girl. Time for brekky?" Zac opened the cupboard and brought out her special food, pouring it into a dish. "There you go."

Ziva barked before diving in.

"Morning," Griff said, wiping his eyes. "You're up early."

"Couldn't sleep. However, I'm surprised Olly isn't up." Zac opened his email and ran his fingers down the list, stopping at one from the judge. "Here we go. The judge has signed the warrant. We can pick it up first thing."

Griff took a mug from the coffee stand. "First, I require help to wake up."

Zac winked. "Late night with Skye? How did it go?"

"Good. Well, at least I think it did. I'm planning on asking her out again." He poured the coffee and peered out the window. "Great, it's snowing hard again. This winter has pummeled us already. How did Olive take the news of your real identity?"

"Not good. Listen, I'm sorry for keeping it from everyone. I couldn't risk it getting out."

"I get it, buddy. You did what you had to do." He took cream from the fridge. "How's the chief taking it?"

"Not sure. He's been silent." He glanced at his watch again. Six thirty. "Time to get Olly up. We should bring her to the house. She has a knack for seeing things I don't. Plus, I need her close until we catch JB."

Zac proceeded to her room and knocked, tapping his toe as he waited.

No answer.

He knocked harder.

Nothing.

He eased the door open, peeking his head in. "Wakey, wakey."

The glow from the tiny, lit Christmas tree on Grace's nightstand illuminated the room. Olly's bed covers were ruffled, but she was nowhere in sight.

He had passed the washroom and knew she wasn't in there as the door had been wide open. Zac walked to Grace's bed.

She slept soundly. Seemed his knocking and presence hadn't woken the six-year-old.

"Olly, where are you?" He turned and walked to the bed's other side, stepping on a fallen object. A tingle shot up his spine.

Olly's cell phone. Shattered.

Zac stilled as fear spiked through his iced veins. Something was wrong.

It was then he noticed a single jingle bell sitting on the nightstand, along with a typed note. Zac snatched it and read.

I have your love. You blew your shot with her. She's mine now.

"No!" Zac returned to Griff, holding out the note and bell. "JB's taken Olly!"

Griff slammed his cup down, coffee splattering over the counter. "I'll wake Skye."

"I'm going to search the property." He turned to his partner. "Ziva, come."

Zac called for backup as the team searched the property, just in case JB held her somewhere close, but Olly was gone. Someone had jimmied the back door open and Zac suspected JB had entered after Ziva and he had left to do their sweep before bed. Zac's pulse wouldn't stop its constant hammering at the thought of Olly's abduction happening hours ago. Why hadn't he checked on her sooner?

Lord, save her. I just found her again and can't lose the woman I love.

The chief had arrived, and everyone gathered in the living room. Grace sat at the kitchen table coloring, unaware of Olly's status.

Chief Bennett held up a folded wad of papers. "I have the warrant to search Darla Parsons's property. Perhaps something at the house will be the key in discovering JB's identity and finding Olive. I will leave men here at the house to watch over Grace and Abby. The rest of you are with me." He squeezed Zac's shoulder. "We will find her."

Zac stood. "Let's go."

His mother latched onto his hand as he walked by her. "Son, God's got this. I'll be praying. Find our girl."

He bent down and kissed her cheek. "Love you."

"Stay safe."

Fifteen minutes later, the team approached Darla Parsons's home. The chief pounded on the front door. "Police. Open up. We have a warrant to search the premises."

They waited.

Bennett rang the doorbell and pounded again. Silence.

Bennett turned to Griff. "Breach. We have probable cause Olive is in danger and possibly inside. Plus, we have this." He held up the warrant.

Griff nodded and thrust the battering ram into the door, splintering the wood.

The team rushed in, weapons raised and ready.

Moments later, they'd cleared the entire house. Neither JB nor Olly was anywhere on the premises.

Zac removed his hat and raked his fingers

through his hair, bile rising at the back of his tongue. He plunked himself into a chair and hung his head.

Lord, I can't do this anymore by myself. I need You back in my life. Forgive me for always questioning Your motives and why You allow so much evil into the world. Help me trust You in all aspects of my life, especially with finding Olly. If it be Your will, help me get another shot with her. I love her, Lord.

Ziva nuzzled her snout into Zac's bowed head.

He hugged his partner. "You're such a good girl. Ziva, let's find Olly."

Ziva barked.

Pounding footfalls stormed into the room.

Zac shot up.

Griff motioned for him to follow. "Zac, you need to see this."

"Ziva, come."

They followed him into a chilled basement. Ice snaked up Zac's spine, but he ignored it and proceeded around a corner.

Griff led them to a door. "We found this room locked and bolted with a chain. We figured we'd find something JB wanted to stay hidden. Check it out."

Zac entered, his jaw dropping. Pictures of all the victims lined one wall with X's through the ones JB had eliminated, including Pastor Felix.

Newspaper clippings of JB's mother's arrest, trial, and conviction, including one article about her suicide.

Griff pointed to a picture of Leonard, the paramedic. "This is why he killed Brett's partner. Supposedly, he'd failed to save his mother when he'd responded to the prison call."

Zac whistled. "He targeted everyone involved with his mother's case, but what's his name?" He stepped over to a round table sitting in the large room's corner.

He rummaged through the papers until he found floor plans to a house, grounds, and a swing bridge. "Look at this. Appears like he's been studying these specs." Zac leaned closer and pointed to the address. "I'm not familiar with this road."

Griff snapped his fingers. "Wait a minute. I know where this is. It's an abandoned stone house on the outskirts of town used years ago for smuggling illegal immigrants. It's perched beside an old cemetery, on top of a cliff." He paused. "The road washed out years ago and the only access is over a swing bridge."

Perspiration beaded on Zac's forehead regardless of the chilled room. He not only hated heights but any form of a moving bridge. His fingers shook and he clasped his hands together to stop the tremors. *You can do this.* He ignored his fears and pushed the papers aside, exposing a drawing of a bomb set in a collar. "Look at this."

Griff cursed. "Do you think he's using it on Olive?"

Zac swallowed the lump in his throat and straightened. "We need to get to that house. Now." He spied an old typewriter on the desk in the opposite corner. "This is definitely JB's lair. Just wish we knew who he was. Honestly, I don't remember any fellow students with the last name Parsons."

"That's because Darla remarried." Bennett walked into the room, thrusting a marriage certificate in his hands. "Recognize her former last name."

"Rogers."

Zac sucked in a breath. The Jingle Bell Bomber was his hockey buddy, Sebastian Rogers—also the station's electrician. No wonder he had easy access to their information.

And Zac now remembered the obsessed crush Sebastian had had on Olive Wells in high school. His end game involved Olly. She was the last person on his naughty list.

"Ziva, come." Zac raced up the stairs.

He had to save the love of his life.

Olive struggled to open her heavy eyelids as a mildewy smell assaulted her nose, sending dread into her limbs and weighing her down. A cement surface beneath her chilled her to the bone. Tightness circled her neck. What was that? She fingered the object before pushing herself upright. Without a mirror to confirm, she guessed it to be a choker of some type with a jingle bell hanging from it. She peered around the room. Where was she? It appeared to be some sort of dungeon-like stone room. Her cement bed was attached to the wall. Who brought her here?

Then she remembered.

The needle plunging into her neck as she saw JB's face clearly. The man's identity had come to light just as darkness had overtaken her and before she could cry out.

Tremors tormented her body and she wrapped her arms tightly around her belly to subdue her terror. A panicked thought entered her mind.

I'm about to die.

Tears formed and rolled down her cheeks. Tears laced with regret over her broken relationship with Zac and her father. She rubbed her abdomen. Most of all, regret of never having a child form inside her.

Forgive. The word popped into her head. She now realized she had to not only forgive her father and Zac, but God. She had clung to the past for too long and blamed Him for her loss and for her fear of never wanting to get pregnant.

I'm sorry, Lord. I shouldn't have blamed You for my miscarriage, but trusted You had a plan despite the loss. Forgive me for my mistrust and my fears. Forgive me for keeping my secret all these years. She held her palms up, holding out her arms. *I surrender my life and everything in it to You. Now and forever. No matter how long that is.*

Tears tumbled down her cheeks as peace filled her body. The verse from Romans entered her mind and reassured her God did work out good for His people. They only had to trust He was in control, not them.

The door scraped open, interrupting her surrender.

"You're awake. Welcome to your new home." Sebastian Rogers stood before her, holding a tray in one hand and a tablet in the other. "Hungry?"

She folded her arms. "Where's Grace?"

"Oh, I assure you, she's okay. You were the one I wanted to end my game." His eyes softened. "I don't kill children."

"Because you have a soft spot for them after years of being mistreated by Principal Bell and Brad?"

"Smart girl. They paid the price." He set the tray of fruit on the cement table in the corner along with his tablet.

"How did you find us and get into the house without being detected?"

"Being Stittsrock Falls police station's electrician gave me access to everything. I snuck into the house when Zac and Ziva went outside." He hauled over a metal chair, it scraping on the stone floor. He sat. "What you all don't know is, throughout the years of being rejected by everyone, I honed my skills. Figured out how to build bombs, become a hacker, and an excellent shot."

"So this all started long before your mother's conviction and suicide."

"You figured it out. Good girl." He leaned forward, clasping his hands together. "Yes. It actually started in high school after every girl I ever asked out rejected me, including you. Of all of them, your rejection hit me the hardest." He ran his index finger down her cheek.

She recoiled against the stone wall, distancing herself from his touch. "Leave me alone." His obsession with her flashed back into her mind. She had turned down his invitation to attend their prom together. Something in their friendship had shifted, but she'd thought he had changed in more recent years. "Don't you go to hockey games with Zac?"

"Yes. I was desperate for friendships, so I faked my Christianity and the boys accepted me with open arms. Fools."

"Why this deadly jingle bell game and naughty list?"

His face twisted into an evil sneer. "Payback and justice for everyone who wronged me. My sweet mother didn't deserve to be convicted of a crime she didn't commit. She did not kill her sister. I had to share her story by eliminating those responsible, and Christmas was the perfect time to do it, especially because she died last year on December 25. I've been planning my revenge for a year, creating my list."

"Whether or not your mother was guilty, those people didn't deserve to die."

"She was not guilty!" He waggled his finger in her face. "And don't tell me what they deserve."

She tugged at the choker around her neck. "And why do I deserve this? I'm guessing it's rigged with an explosive?"

"You're not only beautiful, but smart." He got up and walked to the one tiny window on the stone wall. "Once my jingle bell plan formed, I knew I would use you and Zac. You for rejecting me and him for stealing you from me. I also required your help to give me the recognition I needed. You see, I never planned to kill you until now. You and Zac are the final pawns in my game."

"You're sick."

An alarm sounded on his tablet. He picked

it up and swiped the screen. "Seems like your friends found my mother's house and my secret hideout here. I put motion detectors by the bridge connecting this area to the house." He clicked a button.

The choker on her neck buzzed before beeping.

"The game is about to end—for all of you. I must go tend to my guests. I have something special planned for them." He opened the door but turned. "Oh, and don't leave. The minute you walk through the door, the bomb will explode. Merry Christmas." He slammed the sturdy oak door shut, the sound of it bolting and locking her inside followed.

Her heart pounded with every beep of the deadly jingle bell choker around her neck.

Lord, save Zac and help Grace find her forever home.

Zac stopped in his tracks at the swinging bridge's edge linking the cavern between the washed-out road and the cliff containing the cemetery and stone house—Olly's prison. Snow had covered the walkway from the storm that had moved in overnight. Zac gripped his hold on his weapon tighter. He had to get to her and if it meant crossing the rickety bridge, he would do it.

For her.

"We have to cross one at a time just to test how

strong the bridge is." Chief Bennett had been cleared at the hospital and now motioned for the Emergency Response Unit, including Pike, to come forward.

"When do you think they constructed this?" Zac asked, fearful of his chief's assessment.

Griff held up his tablet. "I can tell you that. I just confirmed the road washed out thirty years ago, according to this article I found, after an earthquake had severed the crossing and made the property its own stand-alone entity. The cemetery keeper had abandoned it at the same time, and a smuggling ring built the bridge to use it for bringing in immigrants."

"So it's the perfect place for Sebastian to hide Olly." Zac couldn't believe his "buddy" had fooled all of them.

"We'll get the unit to proceed first," Bennett said.

"No, let me and Ziva do it. She'll search for bombs before you guys cross. She's faster." Zac had to do this for Olly.

"Stand down," Pike said. "Let me go. I'm more experienced in explosives."

"Not happening," Zac turned to Ziva. "Come."

Give me strength, Lord. Keep my fears at bay. Zac inhaled deeply and clasped the railing with a viselike grip, gingerly stepping onto the wood plank to test its strength. It held, so he continued, one step at a time. He and Ziva made it to the other side without difficulties. He depressed his radio button. "It's good. You can proceed."

Ziva barked and growled.

Something had caught her attention.

An RPG exploded into the bridge's other side, severing Zac and Ziva from the rest of the team.

"No!" He hit the button. "Report, report."

"Zac, the explosion threw the chief backward, but he seems to be okay," Griff said. "The bridge is ruined. We'll search for an alternate route, but for now, you're on your own."

That meant there was no other way back— and—Sebastian had been watching.

He was about to finish his jingle bell game.

Lord, don't let this maniac get away with this. Help me find Olly.

Zac adjusted his bag across his shoulders. "Ziva, come." He rushed toward the stone house, scanning the best possible entrance. Choosing the side door, he tested the knob. Unlocked. Of course it was. JB wanted him to enter. It was all part of his end game.

Zac raised his Glock and yanked the door open.

The song "Jingle Bells" played somewhere in the distance. Zac guessed that was the clue to what direction he was to take. Dare he play right into JB's hands?

He had no other choice, but he'd trust in God and the partner beside him.

Zac withdrew his flashlight and unfastened his K-9's leash. "Ziva, tr-aaa-ack." He stretched out the word, giving her the signal to find Olly.

The dog bounded through the dingy, musty hall and turned a corner. Zac followed, raising both his light and Glock.

He caught sight of Ziva heading down a winding stone staircase. Great. Just where Zac wanted to go—the house's dungeon. Images of the school's basement entered his mind. *No wonder JB—Sebastian—had picked this spot.*

An obvious fitting place to make his final play in his sinister game.

Zac hugged the wall, which was lit with torches, reminding him of a movie, and descended the steps.

Reaching the bottom, he looked left then right. Where had Ziva gone?

Her bark answered his unspoken question. Zac hurried down the right corridor, toward his partner.

Ziva sat in front of what appeared to be an old prison cell. He shone his light on the opposite side. More cells lined the hallway. *What was this place used for?*

Zac inspected the passageway and, after finding it empty, approached the door. "Olly, are you in there?"

"Zac! Be careful. I have a bomb around my neck and JB is nearby. Did you know it's Sebastian?"

"Yes, we figured that out." Zac fingered the chain looped through the door. "Stand back, Olly. I need to shoot the lock to get in."

"Okay. Hurry. I don't know how much time I have left."

Zac stood to the right of the door and motioned to Ziva. "Stay."

He pointed his Glock and fired two shots.

The lock shattered. Zac extracted the chain and tugged open the door, stepping inside.

Olly flew into his arms. "You came for me."

"Of course I did." He held her tight.

The collar around her neck beeped rapidly.

He pulled back and gasped. "The choker is now showing a digital clock. Ten minutes."

"He's been watching. I think he has cameras set up all around as he knew when you approached." She broke away from his embrace. "You and Ziva must leave now."

He grabbed her hand. "You're coming too."

She recoiled. "I can't. He told me the minute I cross the entrance with the collar, the bomb explodes."

"Why you, Olly? You didn't convict his mother."

"No, but I rejected him back in high school and he never forgot it. He's been using me to achieve his game and ultimately it gave him recognition in the media."

Zac holstered his gun, took off his bag, and dropped to the ground, unzipping it. "I have to get the choker off you."

She squatted in front of him, lifting his chin. "Please, save yourself and Ziva. Go."

"Weren't we just in this same predicament? I told you then what I'll tell you now. I'm. Not. Leaving. You." He withdrew a tiny screwdriver and wire cutters from his bag.

"Zac, I need to tell you—"

He placed his finger over her lips. "Tell me after I disarm this." He shone the light around the device, searching it quickly. "I wish for once Pike was here."

"You've got this. Remember your training."

"Right." He pointed. "Sit in that chair."

She obeyed.

Zac motioned to his K-9 to leave. "Ziva, go." He wanted her out of the room.

But, Ziva planted herself beside Olly as if proclaiming to be her protector. She wasn't leaving either.

Zac ran his finger under the choker, circling

around her. "Okay, no trip wires." He squatted in front of her. "I'm going to remove the tiny casing from the digital reading. Stay as still as you can."

He gently unscrewed the plate. "Okay, I see three wires." He racked his brain to determine what his training told him. After examining each wire, he determined how he needed to proceed. "This seems too easy. Pray I cut the right one. Here we go."

They both gulped in a simultaneous breath.

He prayed, tugged out the red wire and snipped it.

The countdown stopped and the latch holding the choker released. He pulled it off and tossed it aside, hauling her into his arms. "It's done. You're okay. We're okay."

"Why would he make it that easy?"

Zac stiffened. "Unless he—"

Ziva growled and jumped to her feet.

"Welcome to the party, Zachery." Sebastian stood in the doorway, gun in hand and pointed directly at them.

Zac sprang to his feet. "You wanted us all here, didn't you? Why not just detonate the device?"

He waved his free arm around. "And ruin this lovely hiding place? Hardly. I have plans— big plans—for this spot." He motioned to Ziva. "Don't worry. I will not hurt that lovely creature. I promise I'll take good care of her." He kept his gun arm raised and walked over, retrieving Zac's Glock from the holster. He tossed it outside the room.

Zac had to act quickly, get the upper hand. "Tell me, why did you worm your way into our lives again, if only to kill us?"

"Oh, I needed friends to occupy my boring life. You, Brett and Mitchell did just that. Loved our hockey games. You guys…not so much. I hated you all for your perfect lives. After Mom died, I knew I would get back at you, so I moved into her home and kept it all a secret."

"Why didn't you tell us your mother was in trouble? We could have helped." Zac wiggled his fingers to get Ziva's attention so he could give her a silent attack signal. Something he alone had trained her to do. He felt her edge closer to him.

"You were all wrapped up in your own little world and—" An alarm sounded, interrupting him. He fished out his cell phone using his free hand and cursed before stuffing it back into his pocket. "How did he find that secret entrance?"

Griff?

Pounding footsteps sounded above them.

It was enough of a distraction to get Ziva to act.

Zac once again wiggled his fingers at his side before pointing his index finger at JB—his silent signal to Ziva.

Zac pushed Olly to the right.

She stumbled to the floor.

JB raised his gun toward Olly.

"No!" Zac yelled.

Ziva bolted, leaping through the air and knocking JB's arm.

The gun fired, but the bullet crashed into the window before the weapon clattered to the stone floor.

Griff appeared in the doorway, his rifle raised. "Stand down, Rogers. Your jingle bell game is over, bomber." He turned to Zac. "You guys okay?"

"Yes, how did you find us?"

"There's an old hidden entrance leading to a tunnel on the property's other side. I radioed to the team. They're on their way." Griff shoved Sebastian to the wall and cuffed him. "Let's go." He tugged the Jingle Bell Bomber from the room.

Zac moved to where Olly had fallen, helped her stand, and brought her into an embrace. "I'm so sorry for pushing you, but I had to get you out of the way."

"It's okay. Ziva saved us both."

"She did." He released Olly. "I'm sorry for keeping a secret from you. Olly, I still love you and want you in my life."

Her eyes saddened, and she tugged free from

his hold. "You won't after I tell you the secret I've kept from everyone."

"I doubt that. Tell me."

She moaned. "I got pregnant in college, but kept it from everyone. While visiting my roommate's family in England, I had a miscarriage and almost died on Christmas Day."

"That's why you seemed to dislike Christmas."

"Yes. It also rocked my world and instilled a fear in me of ever getting pregnant again." She walked to the small window. "When we reconnected a few years ago, I felt God pushing me to let go and date you, so I did."

"And then I broke up with you."

"Yes, and it brought back the fear I thought I'd released." She ran her finger along the stone wall as if distracting herself from the pain. "I threw myself into my work but sensed something was missing, so I applied to be a foster mom. Anything to fill the hole in my heart. They finally accepted me a few months ago."

"And then Grace arrived."

She turned, her eyes brightening. "Yes. My lawyer has petitioned the courts to let me adopt her."

He raced to her side. "I love that and I love you—even with your secret. I'm so sorry you went through that."

"After I woke up in this place, I realized I

haven't been trusting God." She let out an audible sigh. "I love His constant reminders, even though I fail to see them. Sometimes they're gentle. Sometimes they hit you over the head with a two-by-four." She paused. "Finally, I surrendered it all to Him. Released my fears. But will you still accept me as I am?"

He dropped to one knee. "I realize this is an odd time to ask this, but I'm not wasting another minute. I love you, Olive Wells. Will you marry me?"

She fell to the floor. "I love you too. I realize now I never stopped. You're my one true love. Now and forever."

"Is that a yes?"

"Yes!"

He cupped her face in his hands. "Good." He leaned forward and smothered her beautiful lips in a gentle kiss.

Ziva nudged her way into their embrace as if giving her approval of their new family.

They laughed and a phrase his mother always said swept through Zac's mind.

God always gives us the desires of our heart. We just need to trust—and wait for Him to show us what they truly are.

Yes, God had indeed worked everything out for Zac's good.

EPILOGUE

One year later

Olive Turner pressed Play on her tablet and turned up the volume. "Jingle Bells" played through the speakers—a song that once brought fear into the lives of those living in Stittsrock Falls, but a year later filled the Turner home with joy. So much had happened in the past twelve months that Olive couldn't believe how the Lord had blessed her. Not only had He given her the husband she'd always wanted, but the courts had approved her adoption of Grace Patterson. Her daughter now giggled and performed a little jig at the song, moving around the Christmas tree in their new log-cabin-style home.

Olive laughed and winked at her husband of eight months. They had both agreed to a brief engagement, not wanting to waste more time apart.

She thought back to the past year's events. The Jingle Bell Bomber—aka Sebastian Rogers—

had been charged and convicted of multiple murders and attempted murders. Both Zac and Olive had been the key witnesses in his trial. JB had glared at them the entire time they were on the stand, but he'd finally confessed to everything and given specific details to the authorities.

Olive had had nightmares for weeks after all the attempts on her life. She had sought counseling to get past her fears related to being held captive, as well as her terror resulting from her miscarriage years ago. God had held her close, and she had finally released her anxiety.

Carson Wells had apologized for blaming Olive for almost getting her mother killed. Olive had forgiven him and they now kept in constant touch, visiting Evelyn Wells together weekly. Zac and Abby Turner had repaired their strained relationship, both keeping their new names. Harry Burns had been convicted on all counts and was now serving time in a British Columbia federal prison.

Zac's chief had healed from his injuries and promoted Zac for his efforts in solving the Jingle Bell Bomber case. Olive's sergeant had approved her request to promote Lauren to co-lead their analyst department. The pair now worked well together and kept in contact via video meetings. Olive eyed Ziva curled up on her bed positioned beside the fireplace. After saving her life multiple times, the K-9 had eliminated Olive's fear of dogs. Their bond was now unbreakable.

"Gramma, come and help me put candy canes on the tree." Grace tugged Abby Turner from the rocking chair, interrupting her conversation with Olive's father.

The duo finished adding the candy, and Grace turned. "Time to light the tree!"

"Let's do this." Zac picked up the remote. "Countdown from five, please."

The group counted in unison. "Five. Four. Three. Two. One."

Zac hit the button, illuminating the tree.

"Yippee!" Grace yelled.

Olive laughed and removed her final ornament for the tree from its box.

"Are you going to share our news now, Olly?" Zac whispered in her ear and wrapped his arms around her.

She held up the tiny baby slippers hanging from a ribbon and rubbed the eighteen-week bulge of her abdomen with her other hand. The baby growing inside her brought a bonus of joy. Her fear of pregnancy lingered in her mind at times, but she'd learned to leave it in God's hands—in His control.

Olive hit Pause on her tablet and the music stopped. She latched onto Zac's hand. "Everyone, we have something we want to share with you."

The room stilled, and Ziva raised her head, eyeing Olive intently. The dog knew the sound of Olive's voice.

"What is it, honey?" her father asked.

Olive turned to Grace. "What would you think of adding one more ornament to the tree, Lady-bug?"

"Yes!" The seven-year-old bounced up and down. "Can I do it?"

"Of course." Olive raised the booties in the air. "Do you know what this is?"

Abby Turner and Carson Wells both let out a simultaneous cry, drawing Grace's attention.

The little girl's face knotted. "It's slippers. Why are we adding slippers to the tree, Mama?"

Zac lifted Grace. "They're called booties and are for a baby boy or baby girl."

Olive handed the ornament to Grace. "Honey, you're going to be a big sister. Would you like that?"

"Yes! Help me hang it, Papa. Close to the top."

Zac raised her higher and Grace attached the booties to the front of the tree before he set her back down.

He moved next to his wife and leaned in. "Merry Christmas, my love."

Their lips touched in a tender kiss.

"Merry Christmas."

Yes, God gave her multiple bomb-free gifts

over the past year, including her amazing family, but most of all—

Her renewed trust in Jesus—the reason for the season.

* * * * *

If you liked this story from Darlene L. Turner,
check out her previous
Love Inspired Suspense books:

Border Breach
Abducted in Alaska
Lethal Cover-Up
Safe House Exposed
Fatal Forensic Investigation

Available now from Love Inspired Suspense!
Find more great reads at
www.LoveInspired.com.

Dear Reader,

Thank you so much for spending this wild Christmas adventure with Olive, Zac and Ziva! I enjoyed adding a K-9 heroine into this story. She saved many lives throughout the book. Zac and Olive both kept secrets from each other while they battled to stay alive. Thankfully, they had each other to help overcome the difficulties they faced. Trusting God works out all circumstances for our good is tough and I wanted to create flawed characters because they're just like us, right? We struggle too. However, in the end, they grew stronger in their faiths when they surrendered their paths to God's ultimate plan for their lives. It is there we find perfect peace.

I'd love to hear from you. You can contact me through my website www.darlenelturner.com and also sign up for my newsletter to receive exclusive subscriber giveaways. Thanks for reading my story.

God bless,
Darlene L. Turner

Get 4 FREE REWARDS!

We'll send you 2 FREE Books plus 2 FREE Mystery Gifts.

FREE
Value Over
$20

Both the **Love Inspired®** and **Love Inspired® Suspense** series feature compelling novels filled with inspirational romance, faith, forgiveness, and hope.

YES! Please send me 2 FREE novels from the Love Inspired or Love Inspired Suspense series and my 2 FREE gifts (gifts are worth about $10 retail). After receiving them, if I don't wish to receive any more books, I can return the shipping statement marked "cancel." If I don't cancel, I will receive 6 brand-new Love Inspired Larger-Print books or Love Inspired Suspense Larger-Print books every month and be billed just $6.24 each in the U.S. or $6.49 each in Canada. That is a savings of at least 17% off the cover price. It's quite a bargain! Shipping and handling is just 50¢ per book in the U.S. and $1.25 per book in Canada.* I understand that accepting the 2 free books and gifts places me under no obligation to buy anything. I can always return a shipment and cancel at any time by calling the number below. The free books and gifts are mine to keep no matter what I decide.

Choose one: ☐ **Love Inspired**   ☐ **Love Inspired Suspense**
                          Larger-Print   **Larger-Print**
                          (122/322 IDN GRDF)   (107/307 IDN GRDF)

Name (please print)

Address   Apt. #

City   State/Province   Zip/Postal Code

Email: Please check this box ☐ if you would like to receive newsletters and promotional emails from Harlequin Enterprises ULC and its affiliates. You can unsubscribe anytime.

Mail to the Harlequin Reader Service:
IN U.S.A.: P.O. Box 1341, Buffalo, NY 14240-8531
IN CANADA: P.O. Box 603, Fort Erie, Ontario L2A 5X3

Want to try 2 free books from another series? Call 1-800-873-8635 or visit www.ReaderService.com.

COUNTRY LEGACY COLLECTION

19 FREE BOOKS IN ALL!

Cowboys, adventure and romance await you in this new collection! Enjoy superb reading all year long with books by bestselling authors like Diana Palmer, Sasha Summers and Marie Ferrarella!

YES! Please send me the **Country Legacy Collection!** This collection begins with 3 FREE books and 2 FREE gifts in the first shipment. Along with my 3 free books, I'll also get 3 more books from the **Country Legacy Collection**, which I may either return and owe nothing or keep for the low price of $24.60 U.S./$28.12 CDN each plus $2.99 U.S./$7.49 CDN for shipping and handling per shipment*. If I decide to continue, about once a month for 8 months, I will get 6 or 7 more books but will only pay for 4. That means 2 or 3 books in every shipment will be FREE! If I decide to keep the entire collection, I'll have paid for only 32 books because 19 are FREE! I understand that accepting the 3 free books and gifts places me under no obligation to buy anything. I can always return a shipment and cancel at any time. My free books and gifts are mine to keep no matter what I decide.

☐ 275 HCK 1939   ☐ 475 HCK 1939

Name (please print)

Address   Apt. #

City   State/Province   Zip/Postal Code

> Mail to the **Harlequin Reader Service:**
> **IN U.S.A.:** P.O. Box 1341, Buffalo, NY 14240-8571
> **IN CANADA:** P.O. Box 603, Fort Erie, Ontario L2A 5X3

Get 4 FREE REWARDS!

We'll send you 2 FREE Books <u>plus</u> 2 FREE Mystery Gifts.

FREE
Value Over
$20

Both the **Worldwide Library** and **Essential Suspense** series feature compelling novels filled with gripping mysteries, edge of your seat thrillers and heart-stopping romantic suspense stories.